FOR RICHER, FOR POORER: A REGENCY ROMANCE

LOST FORTUNES, FOUND LOVE (BOOK 2)

ROSE PEARSON

FOR RICHER, FOR POORER

Lost Fortunes, Found Love

(Book 2)

By

Rose Pearson

© Copyright 2022 by Rose Pearson - All rights reserved.

In no way is it legal to reproduce, duplicate, or transmit any part of this document by either electronic means or in printed format. Recording of this publication is strictly prohibited and any storage of this document is not allowed unless with written permission from the publisher. All rights reserved.

Respective author owns all copyrights not held by the publisher.

FOR RICHER, FOR POORER

CHAPTER ONE

"It is as bad as we feared, my Lord." Upon hearing those words, Benjamin Harwood, Earl of Wiltsham, rubbed one hand across his eyes, trying to push aside the worry which had been his constant companion these last few weeks. "Come next month, you shall have very little coin with which to pay your staff. You can retain them for another six weeks at the very most, I should imagine."

"Thank you. I appreciate your brutal honesty." Benjamin looked up and gave a small smile to his man of business. "I do not think that I would have been able to see matters so clearly if it had not been for your hard work."

"And as I come to that..." Mr. Crawley looked away. "I do not think that you can employ me for much longer either. You will have to make a great many changes when it comes to your way of living, my Lord. Perhaps it is time that I seek out another employer."

Benjamin scowled.

"I am determined to employ you for as long as it is possible. I have found my valet new employment rather than lose you. These last few weeks I have only managed to keep myself afloat because of your work!"

"Might I ask?" Again, Mr. Crawley's gaze darted away as he rubbed his hands together. There was a seriousness in this discussion that could not be escaped. Benjamin nodded, and Crawley went on. "I want to ask what your intentions are, my Lord. Do you intend to remain at your estate? Or have you any thought about returning to London?"

A cold sensation ran over Benjamin's frame, and he shivered.

"I have very little intention of returning to London. If I can, I shall remain here and make as many economies as I can – and am I not saving expense if I remain here rather than take the carriage to London? An Earl can hardly be seen in London without his carriage!"

A carriage which I can ill afford at present.

A flicker of a smile caught the man's lips.

"Yes, my Lord, you are. I ask only because I have heard from a friend back in London, who states that your acquaintance, Lord Foster, is well on his way to recovering his fortune. He has a great deal of hope, I believe."

Benjamin's breath caught in his chest as he stared at Mr. Crawley. He had not heard from Lord Foster in some days, but could it truly be that the man was soon to regain his fortune? He knew that Lord Foster had been absolutely determined to do so, but if he was close to succeeding, then that gave Benjamin a little hope as regarded his own circumstances.

"Are you sure?"

"I can assure you it is quite true. You know that I am not a man inclined towards gossip. I tell you this so that you might find a little encouragement."

"I am glad to hear of it, for such news may change things a little," Benjamin mused. "I shall write to Lord Foster this very afternoon so that I can hear from him what steps he has taken thus far."

"Then you may return to London after all?"

"I may. I am certain that the *ton* would not be glad of my return, however. I am quite sure that there are more than a few rumors flying about me."

His wry smile was met with silence from Mr. Crawley, which caused Benjamin to wince. Evidently that was true.

"If I may be clear, my Lord, returning to London to seek to regain your fortune is the only way that you can ever return to your previous way of living. As it stands at present, you are a most impoverished gentleman and that will bring with it a great many difficulties."

"Yes, I am well aware of that." So saying, Benjamin pinched the bridge of his nose. "I shall write to Lord Foster this afternoon and I will keep you informed as to whether or not I plan to return to London."

His man of business rose to his feet.

"I am very sorry, my Lord, for all that you have struggled with these last few weeks. The situation itself sounds greatly disturbing."

"I thank you. It is a relief to be believed, at least. I know that you are doing everything you can to aid me with my situation of poverty, as it stands thus far."

"A situation which we must hope we can change, my Lord."

And with that, Mr. Crawley took his leave and Benjamin sat entirely alone, as he had been for so long. Leaning forward, he rested his elbows on his knees and dropped his head into his hands for a moment, struggling not to give in to despair. It had long threatened him, but as yet he was doing a somewhat acceptable job of managing to ignore its lingering presence.

He reached to ring the bell, in the hope of asking his butler or one of the maids for something a little stronger to drink, only to recall that he had no whisky nor brandy left in the house. He had already been forced to make careful decisions as regarded his present circumstances. An impoverished gentleman could not have such things as the very best brandy and thus he had been forced to economize. It had brought him great pain, of course, but what was to be done? As things stood, his situation was very difficult indeed, and he was close to giving up all hope.

Rising from his chair, he wandered to the window and looked out upon his estate. Was he truly to be the one who would ruin his family situation entirely? Was his name to bear the disgrace of their poverty for generations to come? At times, he wanted to weep over what had occurred, only to remind himself that he had not caused it deliberately. If it was as Lord Foster stated, then it appeared that he had not been responsible for his actions that fateful evening. Not that the *ton* would believe it, however, and their opinion would mean that life in London would be rather difficult indeed.

But I must, I shall go.

Speaking determinedly to himself, Benjamin allowed himself a little sense of hope. Mayhap if Lord Foster was able to recover his fortune, then did not that give him a chance to do the same? Out of the six gentlemen who had been injured that evening, Lord Foster had been the most determined to recover everything and to understand what had taken place.

"Perhaps he has been successful."

Mumbling to himself, Benjamin drew his fingers

through his hair, sending it awry, but he did not care. He had spoken to no one other than his staff these last few weeks, and certainly no one had come to call upon him. Why would they do so now, when they knew him to be impoverished; when there was a scandal attached to his name? Mr. Crawley was correct. There was very little hope for him or his family name unless he could find a way to recover his fortune, and remove himself from this situation of poverty, once and for all.

Resting his hands on the windowsill, Benjamin leaned forward, let out a long breath and let his head dangle. That ill-fated evening had been a very difficult one indeed. He had awoken the following day with a concerned butler standing over him with news of his evident foolishness in a letter written by his solicitors at a most early hour. With horror, Benjamin had learned that he had signed a contract, giving his fortune over to a gentleman of whom he had no knowledge. What was worse, was that he had the name of such a fellow, but when he came to look for him, he could find neither hide nor hair of the man. The name, he assumed, was false, but the fortune, however, was gone.

And all because we did as Lord Gillespie suggested and made our way to the East End of London instead of playing at our usual gambling dens.

He could not recall a single thing about that evening. it was nothing more than darkness that shrouded his mind, refusing to give him clarity no matter how hard he begged for it. The last he recalled, he had been enjoying a game of poker, but after that, there came nothing else. Somehow, in the depths of confusion, he had decided to give his fortune away in its entirety and thus had left himself almost completely penniless. At least he had not been the only one affected, or else he would have been quite lost in despair.

Not only Lord Foster, but five other gentlemen were also in such a situation, having each lost their fortunes that dark night. However, all but Lord Foster had returned to their estates, with Lord Stoneleigh needing to recover from an injury sustained that evening. The rest had disappeared, ashamed, and uncertain as to what else they were to do. The *ton* was no longer their friend, turning its back on them entirely. After all, what could an impoverished gentleman offer any of the young ladies of the *ton*, other than a creeping, grasping eagerness for their dowries? Even the thought of returning to London sent a sharp coldness through Benjamin's frame.

"My Lord, you have a letter."

Benjamin turned sharply, just as his butler came into the room. He had already been forced to reduce the number of servants in his home, but those who remained, he very much wished to retain for as long as he could. *But Mr. Crawley stated that I can only afford them for another six weeks at the most.*

"I thank you. Wait a moment until I see if it requires a response."

Opening up the letter, he read the brief lines quickly. His heart soared high, exploding with a sudden, furious hope which seemed to lend a fresh brightness to the room, his breath catching swiftly.

"There is no reply needed, but you must make my carriage ready at once."

"Your carriage, my Lord?"

"Yes. I shall pack my things and depart within the hour." His voice grew a little higher as he hurried towards the door, leaving the butler to stand in the middle of the room. "I am to go to London, and I have every hope of returning with my fortune restored and my estate once more secure."

He did not wait for the butler's response, but pulled the door closed and hurried towards his rooms, fully aware that he would have to pack his own things, given that he had no servant to do it. That did not seem to matter much any longer, however. Lord Foster's letter begged for him to return to London, telling him that he had found a way forward. Now, there was nothing that Benjamin wanted to do other than make his way directly to London so that he might aid Lord Foster in the recovery of his fortune and, in turn, find a little light of hope for himself.

CHAPTER TWO

"So you are now in your second Season, Julia."

Miss Julia Carshaw lifted her head from her book, a book which she had been pretending to read while her brother had stalked through their London townhouse looking for things to complain about. She had no doubt that one of his complaints would be her. Ever since he had taken on the title a little over three years ago, he had become increasingly irritable, with high demands and nothing short of perfection required.

Julia was well aware that she was nowhere near close to perfection. Not that such a thing mattered to her, of course, but it did to her brother, and she was expected to do a great deal better than she was at present.

"Julia. Are you paying me any heed whatsoever?"

"Yes, brother."

Julia closed her book completely as if to show that she was giving him her full attention. Not that she had any intention at all of giving any true thought to whatever it was he was about to throw at her, but the outward appearance of it would be required to placate him.

"As I have previously told you, you are in your second Season and that is something of a disappointment to me. I had expected you to wed already."

Julia's lips twitched.

"I am afraid that I cannot speak for the lack of suitable gentlemen in London last Season."

"Pshaw!" Her brother's guttural exclamation threw aside her weak excuse. "That is nonsense, Julia. You know as well as I that there were many gentlemen interested in your company last Season, but that you refused to acknowledge any of them. Indeed, did not Lord Comfrey seek to acquaint himself with you? He very much wished to court you, did he not?" A dark frown pulled at her brother's forehead. "At least for a time anyway."

Julia forced her lips to remain very flat indeed. Lord Comfrey had indeed offered to court her, but Julia had quickly dissuaded him of such a desire by behaving in a manner he found most inappropriate. Lord Comfrey expected young ladies to stand quite silently, share none of their opinions, and only smile as a singular expression of their enjoyment of any occasion. Julia, on the other hand, had made certain to laugh uproariously, speak her opinion without it having been requested, and talk at length about her love of horses when Lord Comfrey had already stated that it ought to be a discussion saved for the gentlemen only. Lord Comfrey had withdrawn his eagerness to court her soon afterwards - much to her brother's frustration, of course.

"You will find a husband for yourself, Julia. You shall find him within the next fortnight."

Julia's mouth fell open.

"A - a fortnight, brother?" Stuttering, she threw up her

hands. "That is ridiculous. I cannot find a suitable husband in two weeks! The Season has not long begun."

Viscount Kingston rose to his full height, pulling his shoulders back, and glaring at her as though she had displeased him by speaking so.

"Nevertheless, I have decided it shall be a fortnight. And if you do not Julia, then I have every intention of finding you a husband myself."

The confidence and courage which had been in Julia's soul quickly faded, crumpling away into nothing. Her brother's demands were entirely unfair. He could not expect her to find a husband within a fortnight. Surely that was not the done thing, and would raise many an eyebrow should she find herself in such a position. The *ton* would take note of her haste, and wonder why she was doing such a thing.

Perhaps I can use such reasons to my advantage.

"The *ton* will note such eagerness, brother. They might suggest that –"

"I care not for your excuses!"

"It is not excuses, brother." Rising from her chair, Julia took a step towards him, seeing his eyebrows dropping lower still. The last few years had proven to her that her brother was not particularly fond of her, but she had not thought that he disliked her as much as this! "Our family name will be stained if you demand such a thing of me. There will be whispers long after I am wed, which may well cause you difficulty with finding your own match when the time comes."

She wanted to rail at him, to state that it was unfair of him to demand such a thing of her when he was unwed, but carefully held herself back. There is no need to antagonize him still further.

Viscount Kingston folded his arms across his chest, his eyebrows falling still lower over his eyes until all she could see was darkness in his face. Something within her trembled, but she did not back away, resolved not to do as he said. Instead, she kept her chin lifted and her eyes steady, refusing to be cowed.

"Again, you give me excuses, Julia."

"I give you no such thing. I speak the truth. I am not the only young lady in London who did not wed after their first Season. There will be many of us here for our second Season. Why do you place such demands on me? They are most unfair. Even a month would be a difficult request, but it would be better than a fortnight."

Her brother refused to give her any explanation whatsoever.

"I shall find you a husband, one way or the other, Julia. You have a fortnight."

"I shall not wed whoever it is you choose for me."

She was aware that she was speaking foolishly now, but her resolve to disabuse her brother of any notion of control was strong and forced her tongue into action.

Viscount Kingston chuckled, low and dark.

"I think you forget, sister, that I am the one who holds the purse strings. I shall have order in this family. I shall have decorum and I shall have a sister who is wed and settled so that she can no longer be a constant burden on my daily life, on my time, and on my finances." Julia reared back, horrified by her brother's sudden vehemence. She had always known that he was a selfish creature, but she had never thought, nor heard it, to such an extent as this. Her chest grew tight and painful, her breathing difficult. "You shall wed, Julia. I will make sure of it." The only thing she could do was shake her head in refusal. "Yes, you shall."

Struggling to find her voice, Julia forced her gaze up towards her brother.

"I will not marry whoever you choose for me. I do not care how suitable you may think they are, I will *not* have my choice made for me. You may force me to the altar, but I shall never say the words which will tie me to a gentleman for the rest of my life. Not unless *I* can choose the gentleman."

Her brother laughed, shaking his head.

"Do you truly believe that you have any control here? Julia, what shall you do, if you do not wed? Do you have any resources of your own which would permit you to do such a thing?" His words mocked her, and Julia's skin prickled, her heart beginning to pound. This was not at all what she had expected. "Either you will wed, or you will become a spinster and I shall send you to someone who can make more use of you than I can." Julia shook her head, mute. There was nothing she could say. "I shall give you a month, as you have so demanded, but only out of the kindness of my heart. Otherwise, my dear sister, you will find yourself in church with the gentleman whom I select, and then you will have a choice to make. Either you will marry him, and thereby find a life of comfort and all that is good, or you will choose to become a spinster with no money, no good standing, and no future. The choice shall be yours."

Without another word, he strode from the room, leaving Julia breathless with shock and fear as she sank into her chair. Yes, her brother had become much more irritable these last few years, but she had never expected him to demand such a thing as this of her.

I have only a month.

The thought was a terrifying one. How could she have so little time in which she must find herself a suitable gentleman, else face the wrath of her brother? Would he really be as cruel as to force her into spinsterhood? Her stomach twisted as she acknowledged that yes, he would do so. Evidently, she had been a burden upon him for too long. She had known nothing of this, not until this very moment, but it now seemed that her brother had no wish to keep her in his company any longer. He did not wish to pay for her gowns, for her pin money, or for the fripperies that she rarely enjoyed. It appeared that her brother wanted only to consider himself.

"What am I to do?"

Murmuring to herself, Julia rose from her seat and made her way across the room. The London Season had not been particularly enjoyable thus far, but that was mostly due to the fact that she had very little time for the London gentlemen who cared nothing for her and sought only her dowry. She sought a husband who would show an interest in her company, who wished to hear what she had to say, and who had a kind character. All too aware that such a thing was a rarity for any gentleman in London, Julia squeezed her eyes closed and fought despair. She was stronger than this, was she not? Yes, her brother had demanded it, and in doing so, had astonished her entirely, but when had she ever done as her brother asked? That was one of the reasons for his irritation. To her mind, he was not her father, and thus could not make the same demands as a father might.

And father would have been a good deal more considerate, I am sure.

A single tear slipped onto her cheek as she looked down at the London street. There was very little here that brought her any sense of happiness. Yes, there was pleasant company, but she had struggled to find any particular friendship with any young lady from the previous Season. The young ladies were much too eager to discuss dresses and the latest fashion, which Julia did not find of interest, and gentlemen, on the whole, had no desire to hear what a young lady such herself had to say. A dreadful fear suddenly took hold of her, squeezing her breath from her lungs. What if she could find no particular man to be her husband? If the *ton* was as difficult as all that, then surely the chance of her finding a gentleman whom she considered truly respectable and kind would be nigh on impossible!

Then I shall be a spinster.

Her bottom lip wobbled a little as she drew in a deep breath, telling herself that she was not about to give in to tears.

"Spinsterhood cannot be so terrible a situation, I am sure."

Her confident words did nothing to ease the pain in her heart. Try as she might, she could not pretend that being a spinster was anything more than a dreadful prospect. She would have no happiness. No doubt she would be required to find a situation where she might be able to support herself one way or the other, but quite how she was to go about that, Julia did not know. She had no skills with which to do such a thing as that, and if her brother were to find the situation for her, then Julia had every belief that it would not be a pleasant one. He would do whatever he could to punish her for not doing as he had demanded of her, in finding a husband.

"He has all of the control."

Resting her head lightly against the cool glass of the windowpane, Julia closed her eyes. What was a young lady such as herself to do in this situation? Her brother held the purse strings, and he had every opportunity to demand such things of her, knowing that she could do nothing other than either agree or face the consequences of refusing.

Then perhaps I shall have to do something quite extraordinary.

Julia lifted her chin and set her shoulders, refusing to allow any more tears to fall. Yes, her brother had always protested that she was most frustrating when it came to the fact that *she* would do as she thought best rather than pay heed to his own opinion, but now Julia was glad that she had done so. It meant that she had the courage and the fortitude to find her own path, regardless of whatever blocks he put in her way. He would not be successful in this. She would find her own way forward, in one manner or another.

And she would begin this very evening.

CHAPTER THREE

"Good gracious!" Benjamin's heart was hammering furiously, and he pressed one hand to it as if trying to quieten it somewhat. "That was extraordinary."

"Quite extraordinary, yes."

Lord Foster let out a long breath, then reached out one hand towards Miss Lawrence, the young lady who ought not to have been present at this current moment but had been determined to be so. Benjamin could not help but admire her courage.

"You have given us all hope." Benjamin pressed his friend's arm. "I believe that I was lost in a great deal of doubt and uncertainty at one time, and did not believe there would be even the smallest rescue for us. But now I see it can be done. It *is* possible to regain one's fortune."

Lord Foster nodded.

"I believe it is possible for all of us. We were cheated of our fortunes. They were not taken from us with our willing co-operation. If I was cheated of mine, then you have most *certainly* been cheated of yours. I must tell the other gentlemen as well, so that they can have the confidence to search for those responsible. There is more than Lord Montague working in this scheme, and if they can find the men responsible in their cases, then happiness such as this can be theirs also."

Benjamin tried to smile, but his lips refused to do as he asked. He nodded, looking away, realizing that in this happy moment there was also a great struggle. Yes, Lord Foster had recovered his fortune, but his own was still very much out of reach. For Lord Foster, Lord Montague had been the culprit. Lord Gillespie had also been involved, but he, unfortunately, was no longer of this world. Just who was behind the theft of *Benjamin's* fortune?

"You need not struggle, my dear friend." Lord Foster's voice was a little quieter. "I will rehire your servants. You will have your carriage and your horses and remain in London to live just as you please. I will give you everything that you need."

Benjamin's eyebrows shot towards his hairline, and he shook his head.

"No, you cannot do such a thing. You have your own fortune and in time I will be able to regain mine."

His friend, however, refused to accept this and, after some argument and deliberation, Benjamin had no other choice but to accept. Overwhelming relief settled on his shoulders, and he dropped his head forward, not wanting to display any singular emotion at this present moment, for fear that he might lose his composure. Living in poverty had been a very great trial indeed, particularly when he had been forced to give up his carriage. It had been put away ever since his return to London, for he had been forced to sell his horses and also no longer had the coachman or the tiger within his staff who would be needed to use it. Now, it seemed, he would be able to have such a thing again.

"I thank you. I shall not refuse your offer. You cannot know how grateful I am to you, Foster." He spread both hands. "I will be able to hire a valet again!"

His friend laughed.

"Then I shall be very glad to see you well turned out at a ball at my townhouse in four days' time - and you must continue to reside with me until that time if you so wish. We shall attempt to keep the *ton's* rumors to be nothing more than their imagination. Perhaps when they discover the truth, it will be too late, for your fortune will have been restored to you, and all will be well."

Benjamin nodded but did not say anything further. In a short while, Lord Foster and Miss Lawrence departed the room, leaving Benjamin to stand there alone.

I am to have my carriage restored to me.

The relief was so overwhelming that for a few moments he could not bring himself to move. Everything he had lost was not yet returned to him, but his friend's generosity was enough to make it appear so. He would no longer have to eat only half a meal. He would not have to battle with his clothes, trying to make sure that his cravat was correctly tied. He would be able to return to some semblance of normality whilst at the same time, attempting to find out the truth about his fortune and where it had gone. The only thing he was unlikely to regain was his signet ring, which also had disappeared that night.

Perhaps I should take my leave and make my way to my townhouse immediately.

Shaking his head to himself, Benjamin chuckled and followed his friend. He was being a little too hasty. He would wait until the ball was over before he made his way back to his townhouse. That would allow enough time for everything to settle, and for the situation with Lord Foster to resolve itself entirely.

"There is time," he reminded himself, mumbling quietly as he left the room. "If Lord Foster has managed to achieve success, then I shall too. I must force myself to believe it."

∼

"And my cravat?"

"Quite perfect, my Lord." The valet narrowed his eyes as though searching for fault with his work, only to nod. "It looks quite perfect."

Benjamin nodded, unable to pretend to himself that he was not nervous about this coming evening. It was to be his first night back in society since a rumor had spread about his lack of fortune. Having had every intention of making his way back to his own townhouse once the evening was over, he had been a little disappointed to be informed that it was not yet ready for his arrival. He was to stay with Lord Foster for a little longer – which his friend did not mind in the least - but Benjamin found himself eager to return to his own house.

It will not be for too much longer, he reminded himself silently.

Thanks to the goodness of Lord Foster, in less than a fortnight, he would be able to make his way from this residence, in his own carriage, and go to his own townhouse, where he would sleep in his own bed and have his own servants waiting for him.

And then his work would begin. Armed with what he had learned from Lord Foster, Benjamin had every intention of beginning his own investigation into where his fortune had gone. Whether or not he would be able to recover it, he was not sure, but determination now grew steadily within him every single day. He would do all he could, for seeing the happiness that Lord Foster now had with his fortune restored was enough to convince him that it would be a worthwhile endeavor.

"I believe you are quite ready, my Lord." Lord Foster's valet stepped back. "I do hope that you have a pleasant evening."

"As do I, although it cannot be guaranteed."

Muttering to himself and ignoring the slightly surprised look that the valet sent him, Benjamin made his way to the door.

The ballroom was already filled with guests. Benjamin walked in with his head held high and his shoulders straight. He was not about to shrink back, nor hide away in the shadows. Lord Foster had assured him that the *ton* would believe the guise that they were both shrouding him in. After all, many would have mentioned the fact that they had seen his carriage about town so, tonight, no doubt, there would be news that he had hired a full complement of servants for his townhouse, which was being prepared for his return. No one needed to know, as yet, that he was utterly without coin. It would serve him well until he was able to find his way to restoring his fortune - to pay Lord Foster back every single penny he had spent on his recovery at present. Benjamin had to admit that he felt distinctly uncomfortable in taking Lord Foster's money in such a way, but knew all too well that Lord Foster would not permit him to refuse it, having reminded him on more than one occasion that Benjamin would have behaved in precisely the same way, had the tables being turned.

That coin and generosity was precisely *why* he could return to the ballroom and walk in with his head held high.

The *ton* was a fair-weather friend to him. When he'd had a wealthy and prosperous situation, all was well. But the moment that rumors came of his lack of coin, then nothing good could be said of him. He had endured the first fortnight after his difficulties with great pain and frustration, for he had not been welcomed as he had once been. Whenever he walked into a room, whispers came after him without hesitation. The invitations had become fewer and fewer as rumors of his situation had spread - even though he had never given any credence to such whispers. Now, however, Benjamin found himself growing disdainful of what the *ton* had to offer him. No doubt they would welcome him back into their embrace with warmth and delight, believing that the whispers of his lack of fortune must have been a mistake. He would say nothing to disagree, of course, but his behavior had to be cautious. Whilst there was many a beautiful young lady present this evening, Benjamin reminded himself that he could not form a singular attachment with any of them. He could not allow a lady to believe that he might offer her a future, when he had no coin with which to guarantee that. No, he must remain as he was at present, wearing a disguise so that he might not be rejected entirely, whilst knowing full well that he had nothing to offer.

"Lord Wiltsham. How delightful to see you again."

It did not take long for Benjamin to find himself once more a part of London society. Lady Steerford was the first to welcome him, her daughter by her side. Her daughter had enjoyed four Seasons thus far but had not yet found a husband, because during her first Season a scandal had erupted about her behavior with a gentleman. She had protested her innocence but as yet, no other gentleman wished to pursue her

I cannot permit myself to show any interest in the lady either.

"I hear that your townhouse is being prepared for you. How long will it be until your improvements are completed?"

Benjamin blinked.

"Improvements?"

He did not understand the question, but only a second after those words were spoken, Lord Foster himself appeared beside Lady Steerford.

"Pardon my interruption, but I have just been speaking with Lady Steerford and was glad to tell her all about the improvements to your townhouse. I have been very glad to accommodate you in the interim, although I know that you are most eager to return so that you might see it for yourself."

A light shone in Lord Foster's eyes and Benjamin could not help but grin. It seemed that his friend had come up with a convenient excuse for why he had been residing with Lord Foster for the last few weeks.

"I see. Yes, I hope that my improvements will be completed very soon."

He did not give a specific time, choosing to keep any details – entirely fabricated as they were - to himself. The less he said on this, the better.

"That is most exciting. I do hope that you will hold a ball, or have a soiree so that we might see the improvements for ourselves!"

Lady Steerford's eyes glittered, and for a moment, Benjamin wondered whether or not she truly wished to see his townhouse – perhaps considering pushing her daughter forward as a suitable candidate for his wife – or if she wanted to be certain that he spoke the truth. A laugh broke from his lips, an idea coming to his mind as he did so.

"Alas, Lady Steerford, I am afraid that I can do no such thing. The improvements have been made to my study and my bedchamber as well as to the guest rooms. I am afraid I cannot offer you the opportunity, although I am most grateful for your interest, of course."

"I see." Lady Steerford tilted her head, studying him a little longer, her tone indistinct. "I am certain that you will be glad to return to your own home."

"Indeed." Quickly - for he did not much like Lady Steerford - Benjamin gave her a hurried excuse for why he must take his leave. "Forgive me, but I must go and give my compliments to Miss Lawrence to congratulate her on her betrothal to Lord Foster."

It was a poor excuse indeed, but one that Lady Steerford could not protest. Making his way across the ballroom directly towards Miss Lawrence, he smiled in genuine happiness upon seeing her. She in turn gave him a quick curtsey, and then grasped his hand. They had shared so much, the three of them, and he was delighted that she was now to find happiness with Lord Foster.

"Good evening, Lord Wiltsham. I am very glad to see you."

"As I am you. I see that your recent betrothal has brought a new light into your eyes, which could not be mistaken for anything other than the great love and affection you have for Lord Foster."

Miss Lawrence released his hand but kept smiling.

"You are most kind – and correct, I am sure!" They shared a laugh, only for Miss Lawrence to turn slightly and gesture to a young lady standing just to her left, a lady whom Benjamin had never seen before and certainly had not even noticed. "Might I introduce you to my new acquaintance?"

"I humbly beg your pardon. I did not realize that you were in conversation already."

To his surprise, the young lady, to whom he had not been introduced, laughed and waved her hand.

"Pray do not concern yourself, Lord Wiltsham. I do not mind making a new acquaintance. And I have no frustration at being so interrupted when your kind compliments make Miss Lawrence smile so."

"I thank you." Benjamin clicked his heels together and gave her a small bow. "But my apology remains."

Miss Lawrence held out one hand towards him, speaking directly to the young lady.

"Miss Carshaw, this is the Earl of Wiltsham, one of the finest men in all of England. Lord Wiltsham, this is Miss Julia Carshaw. Her brother is a Viscount Kingston, and they have recently returned to London for the Season."

"Miss Carshaw."

Benjamin was about to drop into what would have been his third bow, only to stop himself from doing so just in time. The young lady's eyes glinted with either mirth or mockery, and Benjamin found himself suddenly eager to take his leave. He could not have an open and easy conversation with Miss Lawrence, not with a young lady such as this present. Did this Miss Carshaw know of what had been said about him? Was she aware of everything the *ton* was whispering about him?

"I shall not interrupt your conversation any longer. Forgive me. I do hope that you both enjoy the evening."

Aware that his reaction was a little abrupt, Benjamin hurried from their company regardless, lost somewhere between embarrassment and discomfiture. He was not quite certain that he liked this Miss Carshaw, with those wickedly glinting eyes. Besides which, she had appeared very forward and had laughed and spoken so distinctly that he found him considering her a little improper.

Unless I am simply determined to find fault with her.

What he did not notice was the young lady watching him as he stepped away, her eyes following his every movement until he disappeared into the crowd and could no longer be seen. For him, however, after only a few minutes, she was completely forgotten, and Benjamin once more bent his mind to the task of returning to society, only hoping that his disguise of once more being a wealthy gentleman would remain intact for as long as he required it.

CHAPTER FOUR

"That was a little abrupt, was it not?"
"I shall admit that it was, which is most unlike Lord Wiltsham. He is not a gentleman to behave in any rude manner, although perhaps, given that this is his first foray into society since he has returned to London, he may be feeling a little..."

Noticing that her new acquaintance did not finish her sentence Julia thought to finish it for her.

"Is he a little overwhelmed, mayhap? Distracted by the many people who have come to greet him?"

"I should certainly say that he is a little distracted." Miss Lawrence smiled, but it faded quickly. "He is an excellent gentleman. I am sure that whatever is troubling him will pass soon enough."

Julia did not hesitate.

"And what is it that troubles him so?"

Miss Lawrence blinked quickly and turned her gaze back in Julia's direction as a spot of color came into each cheek.

"I... I could not say. Not for certain, anyway. I know a

little of his present situation, of course, but that is mostly to do with his townhouse, and I am quite certain that it will be resolved soon enough."

A little surprised at how quickly the lady spoke in response, Julia's curiosity grew all the more.

"And what is it about his townhouse that is so troublesome?"

Miss Lawrence cleared her throat gently and looked away again.

"There is nothing particularly troublesome, I suppose, although it must be difficult not to reside at one's own house during the Season." Pre-empting Julia's next question, Miss Lawrence gave her a quick smile. "He is making many improvements to his house, I believe."

"I see. It is very good of Lord Foster to permit Lord Wiltsham to reside with him for so long."

Miss Lawrence laughed.

"I have no doubt that Lord Foster would be glad to have his friend reside here for as long as he wished. They are very dear friends. I am quite certain that he does not find it a trial in the least."

"Then is there much time left before these improvements are to be completed?"

Miss Lawrence spread her hands.

"I could not say. I am sure it will be worth the long wait, however."

"Indeed." Julia murmured quietly, looking after the gentleman who had just departed. It had not been a sennight since her brother had made that particular demand and she was nowhere closer to finding a husband than she had been before, leaving her to consider almost every gentleman she met, regardless of her own feelings on the matter. "And does he reside nearby?"

Miss Lawrence nodded.

"Yes, he is only a short distance away from this house."

Julia tucked this little bit of information away and smiled at Miss Lawrence.

"He seems almost amiable gentleman. You are fond of him, I think."

Miss Lawrence smiled softly.

"Yes, indeed, I find him a very sweet character and a kind spirit. I am grateful to Lord Foster for introducing me to his very dear friend for my life has certainly been enriched by his acquaintance."

"I think it a very rare thing to find such a gentleman," Julia found herself saying, even though she was not particularly well acquainted with Miss Lawrence. "My brother insists I find someone to marry. But how can I do such a thing when they are all either ridiculous fops or grasping, selfish fellows who only care for my dowry? I think you have betrothed yourself to the only amiable gentleman in all of London - and Lord Wiltsham, for all that he appears to be very kind indeed, is much too taken up with matters regarding his house and its improvements to be even considering matrimony, I might presume?"

"I believe you are quite correct in that. Although I shall only agree with the latter rather than the former." Smiling, she spread her hands to the rest of the room. "Lord Wiltsham is certainly very taken up with other matters at present, but he cannot be the only other amiable gentleman available to you, surely. Believe me, I am aware of the requirement to marry and the strain that can place upon one's shoulders! If you wish, I could introduce you to many a gentleman this evening who I consider to be, at the very least, a decent sort. I should not like you to lose heart, or give up entirely, Miss Carshaw."

Thinking Miss Lawrence was an incredibly kind young lady, Julia immediately accepted her offer. This was not the time to be rejecting any offers of help to form new acquaintances, even if she, as yet, was not fully determined to do as her brother asked and was continuing to search for another plan. If she found a suitable gentleman, then perhaps her other considerations would not have to be brought to fruition.

"I should be very glad indeed. Thank you, Miss Lawrence."

"But of course, come this way and I shall introduce you to Lord Peters and Lord Gilkison."

With a smile, Miss Lawrence led the way and Julia followed, although she could not help but glance over her shoulder towards the side of the room where she knew Lord Wiltsham stood. She had no particular interest in the gentleman himself, but rather in what he might be able to offer her - whether willingly or not. An idea had begun to form in her mind as regarded Lord Wiltsham's absence from his townhouse at present. It could be an answer to her own troubles, and that in itself, she considered, was reason enough to pursue it.

∽

"And have you any news for me, Julia?"

Julia looked up at her brother.

"If you are asking me whether or not I have had any gentleman callers, then the answer, brother dear, is yes, I have had one." She smiled slightly as her brother's eyes widened. Evidently, he had not been expecting her to answer in the affirmative. "Lord Gilkison came to call. We enjoyed tea together, with a maid in the room for propriety's sake, and he has taken his leave. We shall see each other again this evening. Does this satisfy you?"

"It only satisfies me if he puts a ring on your finger and takes you away from this house so that you are no longer my burden to bear," came the stark reply. "It is close to ten days since we made our agreement, is it not? And now you are telling me that you have only had one the gentleman caller within those days! Is he a worthy sort? Is he a suitable match for you?"

Fire lit itself in Julia's belly.

"You said nothing about whether a gentleman would be a suitable match, brother. You have told me that I must only find myself a husband, and remove myself from this house so that you can live your life without the burden of your sister upon your shoulders. Why should you care whether or not he is worthy? Why should you give even a single thought as to whether or not he is a gentleman of quality?"

Her brother lifted an eyebrow, and for a moment Julia thought he was about to respond with either shock or an apology for having treated her so. But in the next moment, that illusion was broken as he began to laugh. It was a hard, cruel sound and Julia shivered but removed herself from her chair so that she was standing facing her brother.

I must remain strong.

"You have not always been this way, Kingston. You have not always been cruel or unfair, and demands such as this are not something I have ever thought to expect of your character. Why now do you treat me in such a way? Why do you make such demands on me and set such heaviness on my shoulders?"

Her questions echoed around the room, and for a moment, she thought that he would turn away from her – only for his eyes to narrow and his lips to curl.

"You cannot even begin to imagine what it is like to have such a responsibility as mine, Julia. I am a gentleman who is forced to bear a title and the heaviness which comes with it. I have an estate to manage and a fortune with it. You may not be aware, but father was not the wisest of gentlemen when it came to his expenditure, particularly in the latter years of his life. I did not put any particular pressure on you last Season to wed because I fully expected you to do so of your own accord, knowing that such a thing is both of importance and fully expected of you. In the months since then, I have seen you wandering about the estate, doing very little of note. You have purchased things that you have no need to buy, spending fruitlessly and aimlessly whenever you please. You required an extra bucket of coal every single day during the winter months and that sort of expenditure is not something that can continue, not if I am to make certain that the estate is profitable for whenever I am ready to pass the title along."

Julia narrowed her eyes. There was something in her brother's manner which told her that he was not speaking the entirety of the truth. Whether it was the fact that his voice had lifted a little, or that his eyes no longer held hers, but darted about the room, she found herself suspicious of him.

"We are not impoverished, brother."

"You know nothing, Julia."

His sharp response cut through her words, but Julia was not about to let him speak, so taking a step forward, she sliced the air between them with her hand.

"I know we are not impoverished Kingston - for you, yourself, have only just purchased a beautiful new pair of greys. There are stables at your estate, are there not, full of the best horses. If we were struggling so much with our coin, then you certainly would not have spent so much money on a pair of horses that you do not require. A sudden realization struck her, and her mouth swung ajar, a pale coolness spreading across her chest as she studied him. "I realize now what it is." Her voice softened, horror wrapping itself around her and squeezing tight. "When I say that you have changed, it has only been since you have taken on the title. I realize now why you wish to marry me off this Season. Finally, you have access to our family fortune. You are the sole owner of every single coin in our coffers. And I see, brother, that you want them all for yourself. You have no wish to spend a single penny on someone such as I, your own flesh and blood. Finally, I realize. You wish to marry me off so that you may keep your money for yourself. Is that not so?"

Her brother opened and closed his mouth, but no response was given. Julia folded her arms across her chest, confident in herself that she had found the reason for her brother's determination to remove her from his household as soon as possible. Her anger and upset were so great that she could not speak for some minutes, and thus a furious silence hovered between them. Viscount Kingston, it seemed, could find no words to come to his own defense, which left the truth sitting on Julia's heart all the more heavily.

"My reasons are entirely my own, Julia," he eventually spat, turning briskly away from her as though he wished to end the conversation on that note. "Find yourself a husband."

"Our father would be ashamed of you for what you are doing." Julia strode after him, one hand reaching out to grab her brother's arm. "He treated me with care and consideration, whilst you treat me with contempt. You have no thought for me, save for what hold I have on your precious coffers. You do not see me as your sister, someone you need to care for, someone you need to show love to. Instead, you see me as a leech, draining the life from you and stealing from your great heap of coins. That is not the responsibility father laid on your shoulders on the day of his passing!"

Her brother shook her off fiercely. His face had gone a dreadful white, but his lips were a slash of red.

"Do not speak of our father to me. I have spent years bearing the title and, little by little, have seen how foolish he was in spending money where he did not need to do so. He gave you and mother so much that he was not required to - mother especially. What he gave her was utter extravagance, nothing more."

At this, Julia fell back, unable to say anything further. The mention of their mother had shaken her to her core. Viscountess Kingston had been the most gentle and beautiful creature that Julia had ever known, who had never had a harsh word for anyone. Julia had never doubted just how much her mother loved her, nor how much she loved her son. To hear her brother speak so harshly of her now was horrifying indeed.

"Our father and mother cared for each other deeply, brother." Her voice was hoarse and shaken. "How can you look back at the memory of them so pitifully now?"

"You think of them much too fondly," he returned, waving one hand as if dismissing her. "My reasons for encouraging you to find a husband are entirely my own. But as I have said, you will no longer be a burden, either financially or otherwise, and that, I can see, will be of great benefit to me, which is my only priority. So either you will wed, or you will be sent to a situation where I need not deal with you any longer... and where you are no longer dependent on my finances in the same way as you are at present. And that, my *dear* sister, is my final word on the matter."

He swept out, slamming the door behind him, and Julia was left staring at it, filled with shock and disgust at her brother's cruelty and selfishness. It had crept up on him slowly, so that she had not recognized the hold it had on his character until this very moment. But now it seemed that, once her brother had taken on the title, the prospect of being in sole control of a vast fortune and having such singular power had quite ruined his character. There wasn't kindness there anymore. The money he had, he wanted to keep for himself, fully ignoring the fact that he had a sister to care for, to the point that he was now willing to dispose of her in any way he could.

Sitting down carefully. Julia put her face in her hands. She did not want to weep, however, and forced the hot tears back from her burning eyes. The idea which had come to her at the ball where she had met Lord Wiltsham came back to her at once.

I have to find a way to run from my brother, to hide from his cruel demands.

She had no desire to find out which gentleman her brother would choose for her if she did not herself find a match within the next three weeks. If she wed a gentleman of his choice, Julia had no doubt that her life would be one of misery, married to a gentleman she knew very little about. At the same time, she had no desire to become a spinster either. That would be even worse for, no doubt, her brother would send her to a situation where she would spend the rest of her days without comfort and very little company, likely as a drudge of a companion for someone just as demanding as her brother was.

Dropping her hands to her lap, Julia spoke aloud.

"Why should he get to determine my future according to his terms?"

Her voice was quiet but determined, the tears were now gone. Lifting her chin, she rose from her chair and strode towards the window, looking out at the quiet London street.

This was her life. To permit her brother to dictate it would bring her naught but misery. She was strong with a determined spirit that she was *certain* could prevail if only she had the courage to do as she now planned. Speaking to herself again, Julia cried out in the empty room, her shock fading as fire replaced it, building up within her.

"Then if I must find a way to escape, that is precisely what I will do, whether my brother likes it or not."

CHAPTER FIVE

"And thus, your improvements are completed."
Benjamin chuckled.

"Yes, it seems so. I am grateful to you for your quick thinking when it came to that particular explanation in conversation with Lady Steerford."

"But of course." Lord Foster grinned and Benjamin could not help but chuckle. Lord Foster's devious plans seemed to have worked in Benjamin's favor for, over the last sennight, there had been nothing but talk of Benjamin's improvements to his townhouse amongst the *ton*. "In a way, I think I shall miss having you about the place." Sighing heavily, Lord Foster shook his head, in a most dramatic fashion. "Whatever am I going to do without your excellent company?"

"I am sure that you will do very well indeed, given that you will soon have Miss Lawrence as your wife," Benjamin pointed out, making Lord Foster grin. "I am very pleased for you, my friend."

"I am certain that you shall have as much success as I, in time. I know you have only been in London for a few weeks, and it has been something of a whirlwind sorting out my own situation, but what is your plan? Do you have any intention of pursuing matters?"

He nodded.

"I have every intention of pursuing matters. I just do not know where to begin." Sighing, he shrugged his shoulders. "Everything is so very vague. My memory of that night is very poor indeed."

"No doubt because you were given something to impair your mind, just as I was," Lord Foster put in, his smile no longer present and a heavy frown replacing it instead. "When I determined that Lord Montague was the man who had stolen my wealth, I cannot tell you the relief that filled me. You will feel the same when the time comes. I do not think that he is responsible for your loss of fortune, however, but there will be a connection between him and whoever is responsible. Perhaps in pursuing that, you will be able to find the truth."

Benjamin sighed but allowed a small smile to grace his lips.

"Lord Montague, I am sure, will have a good many connections, but you are right that is the beginning of something, at least." A quiet tap at the door told him that the servant had come to inform him that his carriage was ready, and he immediately put out one hand to Lord Foster's. "I am greatly in your debt, my friend. I may still be penniless, but, for all intents and purposes, I appear to be a gentleman of some wealth once more. The *ton* do not look at me with such disdain any longer, and for that I am incredibly grateful."

"I only hope that it will be an aid in your search for the truth," Lord Foster replied, gripping his hand firmly. "And that you have success. If there is anything that I can do to help you, as you have been of such great assistance to me, then I beg of you to inform me of it immediately."

"I shall," Benjamin promised. "Thank you again, Foster."

Letting go of his friend's hand. Benjamin turned and made his way down to the waiting carriage, his steps light. Finally, he was able to return to his own house. Yes, his friend's hospitality had been most welcome and something he could not have done without, but now the thought of being back in his own townhouse brought nothing but joy. Climbing into his carriage, he sat back against the squabs, and let out a long breath of relief. A smile spread itself across his face as the carriage began to pull away. This was all thanks to Lord Foster's generosity, of course, for he still had no coin of his own, and his fortune was still very much lost. That was something the *ton* did not know of, however, and to their mind, he was just as he had always been. It meant that he would not have to suffer or struggle in the way that Lord Foster had done, but he still bore that same responsibility to himself, and to the generations to come, to find out the truth about where his fortune had gone. Perhaps that, in turn, would embolden the others to do much the same.

The carriage ride did not take long, given that his house was not particularly far. Benjamin had thought to walk, but Lord Foster had been absolutely determined that he would not. As the carriage drew up, Benjamin drew in a heavy breath, contentment mixed with uncertainty tying themselves together in chest. What would it be like to once more be master of his own home, albeit knowing full well that he was without any coin or security of his own?

When the carriage door was opened, he stepped out immediately, standing on the steps and looking up at his townhouse. When he had last left here, he had been a man filled with nothing but despair. He had been forced to remove his servants to send them to other employers and had begun to wonder what it was he could sell that would make enough money to keep his estate from crumbling. Mr. Crawley had been a great support to him, although he had quietly suggested that Benjamin consider selling his house in London – which would have left him with no residence in the city whatsoever - but as yet, it had not come to that, thanks to Lord Foster. For a time, at least, Benjamin could live in comfort here in London, even though he had no intention of continuing to do so in the longer term.

That would mean that I would return to poverty and disgrace if I am unable to regain my fortune.

Refusing to allow such morose thoughts to overtake him, Benjamin walked swiftly towards his front door, which was opened for him.

"Good afternoon, my Lord." The butler took his hat and gloves as Benjamin walked inside, looking up at the familiar rooms and finding himself swamped with relief. There was an inexpressible joy at being back in his townhouse. It built in his chest, threatening to overwhelm him at any moment until he feared he would lose his composure. "Would you care for some refreshment, my Lord?"

Clearing his throat, Benjamin glanced towards his butler, considering for a moment as he battled to regain himself.

"Yes, I think I should."

"Certainly, my Lord. And where should you like me to bring it to you? Your study, perhaps?"

Benjamin hesitated.

"To the drawing room, I think, although I shall make my way to my bedchamber first."

"If there is something you wish me to fetch from your rooms, I can have a footman attend to it for you, my Lord."

Benjamin shook his head.

"I thank you, but there is a personal effect I wish to collect, but I shall make my way to the drawing room shortly."

"Very good, my Lord."

Inclining his head a little, the butler quickly took his leave, as Benjamin hurried up the staircase towards his bedchamber. Turning the door handle, he pushed the door open wide and stepped inside.

Everything was just as he remembered. Sighing contentedly, Benjamin took a moment to take it in, a little surprised to feel such relief still, before making his way to the small chest of drawers on the left-hand side of his bed. Opening the top drawer, he picked up the small book which was within and opened it. Within that, there was a small piece of folded paper, and he took it out carefully, glad that he had thought to store it in such a safe location. This written recollection of what had occurred on the night he had lost his fortune was of great importance to him. He had written it in the hours after he had awoken, being certain to write down every single detail so that he would not forget it. It was sparse, but it was better than his own poor memory, now, which seemed to be fading even further with every day that passed. Lord Foster had been able to recover his fortune and encouraged Benjamin now to do the same, so he knew that he would have to give that sparse record all of his attention. Unfolding it carefully, he read the details, rubbing over his chin as he took in his own distressed words. Perhaps there was something in that piece of paper that could lead him towards finding the culprit. Folding it up again, he nodded to himself, thinking that he would take some time later that evening to sit and think, to try to recollect, in case there was anything more he had forgotten.

Holding it carefully in his hand. Benjamin turned around to look at his bedchamber. How grateful he was that he was now back in his own home! It was as if he had never lost his fortune, as though he had never struggled these last few weeks. Had he been at his country estate, he would not have been able to continue such an illusion but here in London that was easy enough to do.

Walking to the door, he stepped out into the hallway, meaning to make his way towards the staircase, only to turn around again. The feeling of nostalgia continued to run through his veins, filling him with a desire to step into each and every room of his townhouse, almost as if he wanted to make certain that they were all still there.

One by one, he stepped into every room of the upper floors. Many of the rooms were under dust covers, with some empty save for one or two pieces of furniture. Benjamin was grateful nonetheless, glad that he could be here.

These rooms will not stay under dust covers for long, he promised himself. *When I have my fortune back, then I shall have many guests, so that we might enjoy company and good entertainment.*

For the moment, however, he had to be very cautious indeed, for he could not spend any money on fripperies. Yes, he could enjoy invitations to soirees and the like, but he certainly could not afford the theatre, for example.

"If Lord Foster can find success, then I shall be able to do so also," he reminded himself aloud. "Soon, I shall be able to have guests residing with me once more."

Opening the door to the final guest bedchamber, he stepped inside, expecting to only glance around the room and then remove himself from it. Instead, his eyes caught on something - or, he realized, some*one* - who appeared to be lying in the bed itself. Was there someone present in his house whom the staff had not told him of? Did he have a guest already? Some cousin or relative?

Clearing his throat loudly, he waited for the figure to move, but they did not. A sudden fear caught him, rolling around in the pit of his stomach. Whoever this was, had they come into his house to find a sickbed for themselves when they had none? Or was this someone he knew, seeking to take advantage of him?

Steeling himself, Benjamin made his way towards the bed. He had no intention of simply allowing this person to remain as they were, relative or otherwise. Dark hair streamed out across the pillow and, after a moment, he saw her chest rise and fall in sleep. *She is not dead, then.*

Clearing his throat again, he looked down and waited, but she did not open her eyes – just as a sudden flare of recognition shot through his chest.

Whatever is a young lady doing sleeping in my townhouse?

His breath twisted in his chest. What if this young lady had plans to force herself into his life? What if she had every intention of forcing matrimony upon him? That certainly would not do.

He looked down at her face, taking her in. She looked rather peaceful, he had to admit, noting the light flush of pink on her cheeks. Her unpinned hair held dark, gentle curls and Benjamin caught himself wondering just how long it was. How was it that he recognized this young lady? Was she someone of his acquaintance? And if that was the case, whatever was she doing asleep in his guest bedchamber?

"Rouse yourself at once." Trying to make his voice fill the room, he spoke with as much strength as he could, but the young lady did not so much as flinch. Instead, she continued to sleep soundly. Stretching out one hand, Benjamin gingerly gave her shoulder a slight nudge. Again, the young lady did not move. Becoming a little more frustrated, Benjamin gave her shoulder a stronger shake. "Whatever are you doing here? Why are you asleep in my house?" Thankfully, this seemed to rouse the young lady, for her eyelashes flickered and, after a moment, she opened them slowly. Benjamin stepped back, finding himself a little caught by the vividness of her green eyes. *Now is not the time to notice such beauty.* Lifting his chin, he folded his arms across his chest. "Explain yourself at once, miss." The young lady stared blankly at him, as though he were asking her something quite ridiculous. "Who are you?"

The young lady's voice was a little quiet.

"You - you have not had improvements done." Her eyes narrowed, as though it were Benjamin's fault for behaving in such a way that had brought her to this present circumstance. "You have told everyone in town that you are having improvements made to your townhouse." She rubbed one hand over her eyes. "But I can see that you are not."

"My improvements have been completed," he snapped, filled with the urge to reach out to shake her shoulder again, for she still appeared to be quite at home and not in the least perturbed that he had found her. "Explain yourself. Who are you and why are you in my townhouse?"

The young lady yawned.

"You stated that you would not be back at your house for some time, my Lord. Might I ask you also to explain yourself?"

Benjamin's mouth fell open. The audacity of this young

lady was quite shocking. He had no cause to give her any explanation for why he was now at home but evidently to her mind, he had every reason to do so.

"Remove yourself from this bed at once." With every bit of strength he had, he forced authority into his voice. "And then you shall tell me exactly what you are doing here, else I shall have no other choice but to demand that my staff take a look at you in the hope that one of them will know exactly whose household you come from."

"I am not a maid," she snapped, pushing herself up, her eyes suddenly narrowing. "Do you really think I would have stayed in this particular bedchamber if I did not have reason? I am a young lady of quality."

"Then if you are as you state, give me your name. This the last time I shall ask you: tell me what it is you are doing here."

CHAPTER SIX

*J*ulia looked into the eyes of Lord Wiltsham and found her stomach twisting in all directions. She had not expected him to return so soon. What she *had* thought was that she would be in a house filled with men hard at work and with a good deal of detritus here and there. She had expected to be able to hide away for a short while, to allow her plans to come to fruition. Instead, she had come to a perfectly well-ordered house where either improvements had been made and finished, or where there had never been any improvements made at all. Yes, she had been able to slip inside without being noticed, but the shock of what she had then discovered had rendered her confused and upset – and then, once she had found herself in a quiet guest chamber where she was not likely to be disturbed, weakness had overtaken her. Sleep, she had thought, would be the thing that might bring her a little peace and perhaps, thereafter, clarity.

Not that anything was going to be an excuse for her presence here. her reasons did not matter, in the face of the fact that she was now in Lord Wiltsham's residence without his permission nor his awareness.

"Speak."

His eyes were narrowed, there was a tight line about his mouth, and his arms were folded across his chest. He did not give the impression of a gentleman who was willing to listen. Pushing herself up a little more, Julia tried to find the words to explain.

"I required a place to hide."

"To hide," he repeated as Julia nodded. "To hide from what?"

"To hide from my brother, my Lord."

Pushing her hair back out of her eyes, she quickly began to hope that her plaintive words would fall upon sympathetic ears, despite his obvious upset.

"I see." It seemed that he was not even willing to ask her why such a thing was required. "So you came here? At what time?"

"Only earlier this afternoon. I was so very confused and a little afraid, that I thought I should rest before I decided what to do next. I took out my pins so that I would not ruin your pillowcases."

"How very considerate." Lord Wiltsham's lips worked, but his frown remained. "So you will not have been missed as yet."

"I cannot go back." Pushing back the sheet, she rose from the bed, her dark hair swinging over one shoulder as her gown fell back into place – albeit heavily wrinkled. "You cannot send me back to my brother, my Lord." She had hoped that putting the gentle plea in her voice would be enough to encourage him to at least listen to her, but the frown which lingered across his eyebrows now offered her very little hope. "You must understand, I–"

"I need to understand nothing. You are in my guest bedchamber. You are in my *house!* You have not been invited and if you remain, there will be considerable difficulty which will follow. I will not have you forced into matrimony with me, if that is what your intention was."

"I have not come here in the hope of finding a husband." A tightness began to curl around her heart as embarrassment shot waves of heat into her core. "I did not think you would be returning, as I explained."

"You thought I would not return. To my own house."

"I did not think you would return any time soon, my Lord." Julia tried to explain, her fingers twisting together as she clasped her hands in front of her. "You were having improvements made. I spoke to an acquaintance, and she did not think that you would make your way back to your townhouse for some time. You must understand, I came to this house in the hope of finding a little solace and a little peace so that I might consider what I am to do next to escape my brother's plans for me. I have no intention of returning to his house, and I certainly have no intention of attaching myself to you either. That is precisely what I am trying to escape from."

I should not mention to him the things that I have taken from my brother's house which will keep me in comfort for some years. That might make him think all the more ill of me.

She watched as Lord Wiltsham's frown grew and shadows filled his eyes. He looked at her carefully, tilting his head to the left and then slowly to the right. He said nothing. Julia opened her mouth to express herself once more, but chose wisely to close it again. There was no other explanation she could give beyond what she had already said.

What Lord Wiltsham would do thereafter was his own decision.

"I am afraid that I must ask you to leave my house, at once, given that my servants will no doubt see you present and think the worst, should you linger. I shall not have rumors spread in London about us."

"And what if I do not wish to?"

Fear mounted in her heart, but Lord Wiltsham only rolled his eyes.

"I do not think that you have any right to demand anything of me. You have not been invited into my home and now, you must remove yourself at once." Turning he made his way back to the door. "I will make my way to the drawing room to seek a little refreshment. When I return, I fully expect you to be out of my townhouse and back with your brother where you belong."

Julia came towards him suddenly, a great fear filling her.

"Pray, do not force me back to his house, my Lord." Her hand caught his, pulling him back towards her. "I cannot. I cannot go there. You are forcing me back into a desperate situation where I must wed!"

"I am afraid that I can have no interest in your predicament, although I can think of worse things than being given a husband. I am sure that there are many young ladies who would wish to be given such a thing. Perhaps you should be thanking your brother for his consideration in making certain that you have a happy future ahead of you, for to know that you will be in security and safety is not something to be mocked nor rejected, as far as I am concerned." Tugging his hand away, he once more made his way towards the door. "Good afternoon. I do not think we shall see each other again."

Julia stared after him as the door closed, her heart

pounding furiously. She had not expected Lord Wiltsham to, first of all, come into the room and, secondly, to be so hard-hearted. Had not Miss Lawrence said that he was the very best of gentlemen? Why would he then force her back into a situation where she had no hope?

Because he does not know of it. He did not understand truly what my situation is. I should not expect him to be kind and generous towards me, particularly when I am in his townhouse without his permission. He fears that I seek to force his hand in matrimony.

Her head dropped forward, her hair swinging as she took in a breath. It seemed that she had failed at the very first juncture. She had thought that she would make her way to Lord Wiltsham's empty townhouse and be nothing more than a shadow, ignored by those working within it given that she had dressed in a very simple, drab gown. From here, she would find a way to remove herself from London and set up home elsewhere. That idea had come to a sudden stop when she had realized that there were no improvements, or that those which had been done had already been completed. Having dodged the servants thus far, she had hurried upstairs, found herself in a bedchamber and had closed the door. It was clearly one reserved for guests and she did not think that anyone had set foot within it for some time, given the dust covers over some furniture. Not knowing what else she was to do, and weak with fright and confusion, she had lain down, having every intention of resting for only a short while. A quick glance at the clock on the mantlepiece told her that she had been asleep for many hours.

"And I do not know what my brother will say."

Murmuring aloud, Julia rubbed one hand over her eyes. There was nothing else for her to do, for she could not linger here. Even if she wished to try and hide away, no doubt Lord Wiltsham would send his servants to search the house from top to bottom to make sure that she was not present. She would have to tidy up her hair, gather the few things she had taken with her – the precious items included - and return to her brother's house. No doubt he would ask her where she had been. She would have to think of some excuse.

Tears burned in her eyes as she gathered up her hair. Her first thought had to be to escape her brother's household, and thus far at least she had been successful. She had assumed that she would have time to make further plans as regarded a new life for herself once she was safely ensconced in Lord Wiltsham's home, able to steal food from the pantry late in the evening and hide away in a comfortable room during the day. Returning to her brother very much felt as though she were walking back into captivity. But she had no other choice.

∼

Her brother's house was quiet as Julia slipped back inside. The butler gave her a small but discreet nod, not speaking her name nor any word in fact, evidently fully aware that her brother might be very angry with her should she be discovered. That, at least, was something she was grateful for. Her brother's staff were always considerate of her needs which, in this case, might protect her from Kingston's wrath.

Hurrying to her bedchamber on almost silent feet, Julia reached it without being disturbed, opening the door, and stepping inside. The silence greeted her with great affection, and she closed her eyes tightly, leaning against the door as she did so. Good fortune had been her guide, allowing her back to her room without being noticed – which could mean that she might pretend that she had been here for many hours. Mayhap even her brother would not have noticed her absence.

Tears sprang into her eyes as she considered her failed attempt at escape. There were some things she would have to return before her brother noticed that they were missing. She had been present in his study on many occasions – enough to know where he kept items of particular value and where the key to open their hiding place was. When her brother had been fast asleep the previous evening – having enjoyed an evening in society – she had managed to find the key, open the chest, and pick up the items within. There had been only a few, but she had been relieved to discover that they were of enough value to provide enough money for her to live in comfort for some years, regardless of where she had found herself. The only thing she had returned had been the diamond necklace, for it was a family heirloom and practically priceless. Julia dared not think what her brother would do if he discovered that the necklace was gone and thus, she had returned it to the locked chest in her brother's study.

She blinked rapidly, and a single tear fell to her cheek, but she dashed it away quickly. Could she truly give up and allow her brother to dictate her future? Did she not have enough determination and fierceness to refuse him a little longer? Somehow, she had to find a way. This was her only moment, for if she did not contrive an escape now, then she would either find herself trapped in marriage or spinsterhood, and she did not relish either of those prospects.

"Lord Wiltsham does not appear to have as fine a character as Miss Lawrence indicated." Muttering furiously to herself, Julia scrubbed at her eyes again, all too aware that she was speaking foolishly again, for what gentleman would respond well to a strange young lady asleep in one of his bedchambers, having arrived without permission? At that moment, in explaining herself to him, she had held out one flickering hope, but he had dashed it all too quickly. "What if he could be my only hope?"

A sudden idea came to her mind and Julia could not immediately remove it. If she was forced into it, if she could find no other forward path, then could Lord Wiltsham be the gentleman that she would wed? Miss Lawrence was perfectly convinced that he was the best of men, and for a lady to speak so well of him said a great deal about his character. She would have to discover the truth of his character for herself, of course, but if it came to it, was he a gentleman that she could tie herself to?

Julia tried to dismiss the thought, but it would not leave her. He was the only gentleman of whom she knew anything. If Miss Lawrence was as certain of his character as Julia believed, then she would be a fool not to consider him.

Although that would require his agreeing to marry you.

The awareness of his likely response to her suggesting such a thing to him made a wry smile pull at her lips. Would Lord Wiltsham have any real interest in marrying her after she had done such a thing? Their betrothal would have to be soon if she was to fulfill her brother's demands.

"But my situation is so desperate that I may be forced to take measures which I would never otherwise consider," she murmured to herself. Walking across the room, she went to a chair next to the cold hearth. Her legs wobbled and she sat down quickly, gripping the arms of the chair as a wave of weakness stole the strength from her limbs. Her determination would do nothing in the face of her brother's strength, and even though she had been telling herself that she would find a way past her brother's schemes, what would happen if she could not? If she refused to stand up in church and agree to marry whichever gentleman he had chosen for her, then she would still be at his mercy. Her courage would do nothing for her then. "Then can it be that my only hope is Lord Wiltsham?"

It seemed suddenly strange, but the idea would not leave her. Sitting forward, Julia buried her head in her hands and let the tears fall. All that she had hoped for was crumbling into dust. His return had ruined her plans entirely, to the point that she now had to face a future where she would have to make a decision - either she would have to wed or face spinsterhood at the mercy of her brother's choices, regardless of what she wanted for her life. Sniffing, Julia pulled out her handkerchief and dabbed at her eyes. What was she to do? To do nothing would make her even more miserable than she was at present. She would have to speak to Lord Wiltsham as soon as possible, for if he was as good a gentleman as she hoped she might believe him to be, then she would have to consider him in great detail

And if he was not, Julia did not know what she was to do.

CHAPTER SEVEN

"How do you fare with your consideration of Lord Montague?"

"In truth, I have not given it much thought." Seeing his friend's eyebrows shoot upwards, Benjamin shrugged. "It has only been two days since I have returned to my townhouse, and I have had another matter capture my thoughts."

"Surely it cannot be more important than to find out who has stolen your fortune!"

At this Benjamin winced.

"Yes, you are quite correct. I have allowed myself to become distracted."

"It is just as well, then, that I have found something to aid you."

Lord Foster plucked something from his pocket and handed it with a flourish to Benjamin.

"What is it?"

Unfolding it, Benjamin scrutinized the words.

"It is a list. I had my man of business look into Lord Montague's affairs. These men are all closely acquainted with him."

Benjamin's heart skipped with a surge of anticipation.

"That is very good of you, Foster. You cannot know how much this means to me."

Lord Foster chuckled, but it was not a sound of mirth.

"Believe me, my friend, I know all too well your circumstances at present. It is as though you are grappling in the dark, searching for even the smallest light of illumination; struggling against a lack of hope that burns against your skin a little more with every single hour that passes you by. I can only pray that this will bring you a little encouragement."

"It will do more than that, I can assure you." Benjamin glanced at the six names on the paper. "This is a beginning where I had none."

"Excellent. Might I suggest that you look into whether or not any of them have spent time in the East End where we went that night."

Benjamin nodded.

"And mayhap I shall also see if they were acquainted with Lord Gillespie, God rest his soul."

A frown immediately pulled at Lord Foster's face at the mention of Lord Gillespie, the man who had sent them to the East End of London on the night that Benjamin - as well as the other five men – had lost his entire fortune.

"That would be a wise consideration." Lord Foster tilted his head for a second, his eyes suddenly flickering. "What is it that you remember about that night?"

Benjamin shook his head.

"Very little. I recall that we were all in great spirits, looking forward to an evening of entertainment and joviality. Lord Gillespie suggested that we went to the copper hells in the East End of London, given that we had never been there before, and implied that we might do particularly well. Since many of us were already a little in our cups, we found ourselves there, although Lord Gillespie did not join us, from what I recall.

"He led us there," Lord Foster reminded him, "but did not linger. I can remember very little after that."

"Nor can I." Benjamin rubbed one hand over his forehead. "I wrote down a few details after I woke the morning after that night and what I wrote is only a little helpful. I wrote that there was something which left my brandy tasting a little sour and that, try as I might, I could not seem to finish it. I also noted that I thought it an excellent establishment. I have vague recollections of sitting down with a few others to play a game of cards, but thereafter I remember no great detail. My last memory comes much later in the evening, from when I found myself being poked and prodded by another gentleman – I do not recognize his face – who had me sent to my carriage. On returning to my house, I discovered my servants in uproar in the early hours of the morning. News had reached them that I had handed over my entire fortune to another gentleman. I was quite sure it was nothing short of preposterous. But my solicitor confirmed it to be true. Apparently, a contract was signed at the gambling table."

"And do you have a copy of that contract?"

"I do – my solicitor made a copy, for our records, when the original was presented to him. Of course, it is in his clerk's hand, so it is of little help to us in finding the gentleman who wrote the original. But through that contract, I have signed my fortune over to a Baron March. However, a quick search of the latest edition of Debrett's by my solicitors, and a few well-placed questions to the best gossips in London, indicates that there is no such fellow. Not that it matters. The man now has my funds, and I highly doubt he will be returning them." His shoulders lifted. "I confess myself to be lost in uncertainty, and struggling against a noose of hopelessness. I do not think that I will ever be able to regain my fortune, given that the fellow who has stolen it is not truly as he appeared."

"Do not give up hope. I believe Lord Montague is the fellow who arranged much of what happened that evening, and the one who has pushed everything forward - although he has other gentlemen involved, I am sure. This 'Baron March' will not be far from London. I have no doubt that these nefarious gentlemen have every intention of continuing on as they are, taking whatever fortunes they can from other unfortunate souls who are foolish enough to take themselves to the East End of London solely on one man's recommendation."

"We did not do anything wrong." Refusing to allow any sort of guilt to edge over his soul, Benjamin swiped the air between them. "We were foolish, yes, but we did not go there with the intention of being swindled. You are right that I ought not to give up hope. I have very little of it, but I have some, and that must be enough for the present."

Lord Foster nodded and gripped Benjamin's arm for a moment.

"You will not find yourself struggling in poverty regardless. You know that I am here to support you, now that I have regained my wealth."

"Something I very much appreciate." Setting his shoulders, Benjamin took a deep breath. I am determined to regain my fortune, one way or the other, just as you have regained yours. This list has given me great encouragement."

"I am very glad to hear it. I will be as much of an aid to you as I can be."

"I appreciate that, but I am also aware that you have

your own situation with Miss Lawrence to continue with, now that you are betrothed."

At this remark, Lord Foster's eyes lit up, with a smile on his face that Benjamin had never seen before. Was this how one appeared when one was in love? He had no awareness of the emotion, nor any understanding, for he had never experienced it himself on any occasion. A small touch of envy pressed against his heart, but he ignored it. This was his friend's happiness, and he could not be jealous of him for that

"I may be betrothed, but I do not forget my friends. I do not think that Miss Lawrence would ever permit me to behave so, even if I should wish to!"

Benjamin chuckled.

"You are correct in that! Miss Lawrence is an extraordinary creature, and you are a most fortunate gentleman to be able to call her your own."

"Of that I am very well aware." Lord Foster's smile softened a little. "I find myself very blessed."

Benjamin discovered himself to be smiling.

"You may be surprised to learn that I found myself in a situation recently where I may have been forced to wed, had the circumstances been even a little different."

Lord Foster's eyes widened.

"I beg your pardon?"

"Indeed, it is true. Upon returning to my townhouse. I came upon a young lady, asleep in one of my guest bedchambers. I am certain that I recognized her, but as yet I cannot place her, and she did not give me her name. I was foolish enough not to demand it from her before she left the house, at my direction." Lord Foster's eyes widened still further. "I speak the truth, I assure you!" Benjamin continued, seeing the flash in his friend's eyes. "I could not quite believe my eyes!"

"Good gracious, whatever was her reason for being present in your bedchamber?"

"My *guest* bedchamber," Benjamin corrected. "I cannot recall entirely, such was my shock, but it was something to do with escaping from her brother."

"And was she a lady of quality?

"Yes, I believe so. Her manner and her speech spoke of it. Her hair was unpinned however, which gave her something of a…"

Benjamin trailed off, struggling to find the correct words to describe the young lady. She had not appeared unhandsome with unpinned hair. Rather, he had found it somewhat alluring.

"A little unkempt perhaps?" His friend suggested, and Benjamin nodded fervently. "And did she say what exactly was her situation with her brother?"

Benjamin shrugged.

"Whilst she said something about her brother, I thought it rather a poor excuse, and I was quite certain that it could be nothing too serious." He laughed roughly. "Mayhap it was nothing more than the fact that her brother had refused her acceptance to a most desired ball."

In response to this, his friend did not smile nor laugh his agreement. Instead, he drew his brows together and shook his head.

"I am afraid I must disagree with you there. If the young lady is risking her reputation - and thereby her future - by coming to reside in another gentleman's bedchamber, then her situation must be of grave seriousness indeed. I do not think that any young lady would risk herself in that way, not unless it was a dire situation."

The thump of an arrow of guilt shooting through his heart had Benjamin recoiling a little.

"I... I had not thought of it that way."

"You say you do not recall her name?"

"No, but I am certain that I have been introduced to her before. I could not tell you what her title was or even the name of her father - or her brother, for that matter. I am quite certain that I have met her before, however."

Lord Foster let out a small sigh.

"I suppose that she ought not to concern you greatly, given that she is not your responsibility - although I do hope that she has not been forced to face any grave difficulties."

The guilt in Benjamin's heart swelled even more and became painful.

"Perhaps I should have asked more of her, but yes, you are quite right. She is not my concern."

Telling himself that this was quite true. Benjamin nodded to himself as if in confirmation, so that the guilt he wore would quickly fade.

"Did she appear to be attempting to force you into matrimony?"

Benjamin shook his head.

"That was one of my first thoughts upon seeing her, but she did not make any attempt to do so and certainly had no eagerness to try anything of that nature – she declared that fact quite distinctly. She believed that I was gone from the house and would be for some duration, having expected there to be improvements work in progress."

Lord Foster's eyes flared at this remark.

"Do you not see?"

"See what?"

Confused, Benjamin looked hard at his friend, who only grinned

"She must have been at the ball where I was speaking of the many improvements to your house!"

In a flash, it returned to Benjamin's mind, and he found himself catching his breath.

"Yes, of course!" As Lord Foster grinned back at him, Benjamin waved a hand, the other rubbing at his chin as he thought. "Of late, I have only been at one ball – which was the one where I discussed the improvements to my house with many a guest, thanks to your suggestion."

"Were you introduced to anyone new?"

In response to his friend's question, Benjamin screwed up his face, trying hard to recall.

"I was rather anxious that evening," he remembered. "I was concerned that the *ton* would ignore me entirely. Yes, I was introduced to a few–"

A sudden mental image of a face came back to him, and he threw one hand to his mouth, curling his fingers into a fist as he tried desperately to recall her name.

"You remember her now, do you not?" Lord Foster exclaimed as Benjamin nodded.

"I recall the lady's face, certainly," Benjamin responded. "It was your very own Miss Lawrence who introduced me to her."

Now it was the turn of Lord Foster's eyes to flare.

"Then I believe that I know exactly who it was, who was introduced to you, for she spoke to me of the one singular new acquaintance she had made that evening." Settling one hand on Benjamin's arm, he looked back at him steadily. "Does the name 'Carshaw' mean anything to you?"

Benjamin's hands dropped to his side.

"It certainly does. I know precisely who was in my townhouse, asleep in my guest bedchamber." His fingers curled tightly into fists as he shook his head. "The young lady in question is Miss Carshaw."

Lord Foster's eyes narrowed slightly.

"And are you quite certain?"

Benjamin nodded determinedly, his gaze drifting away for a moment.

"Yes, there can be no doubt. Miss Carshaw was introduced to me by Miss Lawrence at the ball – and she was also the young lady I found in my guest bedchamber." His eyes went back to his friend. "The young lady who was seemingly terrified of her brother."

CHAPTER EIGHT

"Good evening. Miss Carshaw. Might I say how lovely you look this evening."

She waved a hand, dismissing him.

"Yes, yes. You need not give me any particular compliments, Lord Bullfield. I have no doubt that my brother had sent you in my direction." A quick lift of her eyebrows and the flush which came into his face told her that her consideration was correct. "You need not compliment me. I am all too aware of the *many* young ladies whom you like to keep company with, as well as the recently widowed ladies who have lost their husbands but retained a great deal of their wealth."

"Miss Carshaw, I hardly think—"

"If there was to be a match between us, how much of a dowry has my brother promised?"

Lord Bullfield looked away, and his chin lifted although his color remained high.

"He did not offer me any such thing."

Julia rolled her eyes.

"Perhaps I might suppose, then, that he will relieve you

of a great debt should you take my hand in marriage. Alas, I must disabuse you of the idea that I am more than content to be used as a bargaining chip. Good evening, Lord Bullfield." Without so much as a backward glance, and refusing to stay anywhere near her brother, Julia strode away, throwing aside the requirement for a chaperone. "Lord Bullfield, indeed!"

Exclaiming quietly under her breath, she made her way into the shadows at the side of the room and chose to remain there, leaning her back against the wall so that she would not be easily seen. Lord Bullfield was her brother's acquaintance and unfortunately was well known to the *ton* to be something of a flirt. He was not inclined to court and had never expressed any desire to marry, so why her brother thought that she should be interested in him, Julia could not imagine. Mayhap it was that her brother was becoming rather desperate, knowing that if she were wed, then there would be no long-term financial requirement from him any longer, whereas if she became a spinster or companion, then he would have to do *something* to ensure her meager comfort. For her brother, the former would be far more appealing than the latter.

Her chest rose and fell as she watched the growing crowd. There was only one gentleman she was interested in seeing, and he was not yet present. Perhaps he would not appear this evening, but even if he did not, Julia had every intention of speaking with Miss Lawrence about him, planning to ask her as much as she could about Lord Wiltsham. If she was truly to think of him as a potential husband, albeit against her own desire, and her own will, then she would have to know as much about his character as possible.

Her face flushed as she recalled the astonishment on his face when he had caught her in his guest bedchamber.

He had thrown her from the house thereafter and she had been forced to return to her brother's house without so much as a smile from him. There had not been even a modicum of understanding in his manner, and certainly no eagerness to know of what she spoke - and yet she was not inclined to think poorly of him for that. Had she been in his shoes, then she might very well have done the same."

"Are you standing in the shadows for some reason, Miss Carshaw?"

A quick gasp stole her breath as she turned sharply, staggering forward a little only for strong arms to catch hers, setting her back in place. Fearful that it was Lord Bullfield come to force his attentions on her, she let out a small exclamation of relief upon seeing Lord Wiltsham.

"You appear a little surprised to see me. Perhaps you can now understand my own astonishment when I saw you sleeping in my own house."

For some moments, Julia did not know what to say. She stared at the gentleman, wondering how she was to explain herself. He had not cared before, she considered, so why should he care about her situation now?

"Miss Carshaw?"

"Forgive me, I thought you were..." Closing her eyes, she gave her head a slight shake. "I apologize for the surprise. As I said then, I did not mean for you to see me, or even to become aware of my presence. I thought that you were having improvements made in the house. That was my only thought."

"Then you were genuine in your eagerness to escape from whatever it is your brother intends for you."

Believing that his tone was a little condescending. Julia drew herself up. Did he not recall what she had said?

"Yes, my Lord. It is still something which causes me great distress."

"I am sorry for that." To her mind, he did sound rather genuine, and she looked up at him with faint surprise, her shoulders dropping back. "My friend considers that I spoke a little harshly. My shock overcame me, as you can well understand, I am sure. If you are in grave trouble with your brother, then I must pray you are soon able to find a way out of your difficulties."

Julia tried to smile.

"How very considerate of you, Lord Wiltsham. I am certain that I shall be free from my brother soon enough."

This was spoke with more confidence than she actually felt, but it was the only thing she could say under the circumstances. After all, she was not at all convinced that Lord Wiltsham was in any way concerned with the troubles she was facing at present. He was expressing his concern for her, and whilst she appreciated that, it would do nothing to aid her in her present state. All the same, she considered quietly, this did show that he was a gentleman who, upon reflection, was able to recognize his own mistakes. That had to be a pleasing quality, certainly.

"I should bid you good evening, Miss Carshaw." As abruptly as he had arrived, Lord Wiltsham took his leave. "Might I wish you a pleasant evening."

Julia tried to smile, but found that no words came to her lips in response. She could not have a pleasant evening, not when her brother was doing such things as push Lord Bullfield in her direction. Lord Wiltsham threw her another glance over his shoulder and, for a moment, Julia found herself considering whether or not she found him a handsome gentleman. Such things were not of any particular interest to her, of course, but in this regard, if she was genuinely considering him to be a potential candidate for a husband, and thus a key part of her future happiness, then she would prefer to find the gentleman pleasing to look at. With a crop of rather thick dark hair and eyes which could never decide whether they were brown or green, he certainly could catch her interest, should she permit him to do so. She had not yet seen him smile, she decided, and when he did so, that would inform her as to whether or not he was a particularly handsome gentleman.

"I see that you have been talking to Lord Wiltsham. He is a most interesting gentleman, is he not? Always a pleasure to talk to."

"Good evening, Miss Lawrence." Genuinely happy to see a previous acquaintance, Julia smiled. "You must have been searching the hallway, and then the ballroom itself, to have found me in such a secret place!"

"Oh no, I did no such thing, I confess. It is only that Lord Wiltsham came to speak with Lord Foster and, given that I was present, informed me that he had only just finished conversing with you."

"I see." This was her opportunity, she realized, to speak of Lord Wiltsham so that she might find out more about him. "That was very good of him."

"I think that he knew that I would be glad to speak with you again. Tell me, have you been in London for long? Is this your first Season?"

"This is my second Season," Julia replied, trying her best to keep to the subject of Lord Wiltsham. "Although I have not met very many gentlemen, nor ladies for that matter. Last year, my brother did very little to aid me, whereas this Season he is doing all he can to remove me from his house. He wishes me to marry as soon as possible."

"Oh." Miss Lawrence's eyes widened. "That must be

distressing for you. I can imagine that there must be a great deal of strain."

"There is a little, yes." Unwilling to go into further detail. Julia thought about how she might continue speaking of Lord Wiltsham. "That is why I have been most grateful to you for your introductions to various members of the *ton,* Lord Wiltsham included. I was very grateful to him for coming to speak with me this evening, even though I have hidden myself away in the shadows."

"Yes, you have rather." Miss Lawrence looked at her a little askance. "Might I ask why you have done so? Is there any particular reason? I do not mean to pry, of course. If you have no wish to speak of such things with me, then–"

Julia shook her head.

"You need have no concern on my part. I confess that my brother has encouraged me towards one Lord Bullfield." Seeing Miss Lawrence lift her eyebrows, Julia let out a bark of laughter. "I can see from your expression that you understand exactly who I am speaking of. I sought to escape not only him, but anyone else that my brother deems appropriate. I have long wished to find my own husband, at a time that is best for me, but I do not believe that my brother feels the same way. It must be this Season or none at all."

"You do not mean to say that he would cast you out?"

The horror in Miss Lawrence's voice matched the dread in Julia's heart as she found herself speaking with more openness than she had intended.

"I confess I do not know. My heart quails at the thought of what my brother intends for me."

"Then you must find yourself a suitable husband before he can force your hand. I am sure that there are plenty of gentlemen in London this year who are more than suitable."

Julia laughed, but it was dry and coarse.

"That is precisely as my brother says. Alas, as yet, I have not found anyone suitable, but then again, that is mayhap because I have not been given opportunity. Perhaps Lord Wiltsham might be such a gentleman?"

Making sure to keep her tone light, she glanced towards Miss Lawrence, seeking her immediate reaction, and hoping that she might laugh off any awkwardness by stating only that she had been jesting in her suggestion.

Miss Lawrence immediately frowned, and Julia's heart sank. Was there something improper about Lord Wiltsham? Had she misjudged him?

"I cannot tell you whether or not Lord Wiltsham has ever considered matrimony. For even though my husband-to-be is dear friends with him, it is not something that he has ever spoken of with me."

"But do you think him an excellent gentleman? A man's character is all that concerns me, particularly given the fact that my brother is not a gentleman of any kindness. Money has corrupted his heart, you see."

"And for that I am sorry." Miss Lawrence shook her head. "I speak the truth when I say that I cannot give you any real answers. I would advise you, however, that Lord Wiltsham is presently very taken up with a grave matter of the utmost seriousness. I would not think that he would ever consider matrimony at the present moment."

"I see."

Considering this carefully, Julia bit her lip, finding herself gazing around the ballroom as if she hoped desperately to be able to find Lord Wiltsham at any moment. Idly, she wondered what this great and pressing matter might be, which took so much of his attention, but could not come up with a single idea. A gentleman's business matters were his own affair, she supposed.

"You do sound filled with grave concern." Miss Lawrence touched her arm. "Is this situation with your brother truly that bad?"

I have something of a friend in Miss Lawrence, I think. Choosing to be honest. Julia nodded.

"I do not pretend that I wish it were not so, but I find myself in a great deal of difficulty. That is why I must consider every gentleman in London, wondering whether or not they are a suitable match for me, so that my brother does not carry out his threat to either force me into marriage or make me a spinster before my time."

"Oh, my dear." Putting one hand to her heart, Miss Lawrence's eyes were suddenly a little glassy. "He will not consider anything other than this?" Julia shook her head, suddenly surprised to discover that there were tears forming in her eyes. "And you have no one to speak with about this? There is not a mother or a sister." For what was the second time Julia shook her head, suddenly beginning to realize just how isolated she was. "Then you shall have a friend if you wish it." Miss Lawrence smiled warmly as she grasped Julia's hand. "That will make your difficult circumstances a little easier to bear, I hope, for it is all I can offer you."

Julia nodded, a tightness in her throat telling her that she could not find any strength to speak. She had never been one to make friends particularly easily, but Miss Lawrence was offering her something which she had, she realized, long wished for.

"I should like that very much."

Smiling, Miss Lawrence squeezed her fingers.

"Then we shall be great friends, and you shall tell me everything about your brother so that you do not have to carry your burden alone any longer."

"I would be glad to."

CHAPTER NINE

"Good gracious!" Benjamin strode across the room and shook his friend's hand. "How very good to see you."

"You are a little surprised, I think."

"Indeed I am, but that does not mean that I am not glad that you are here," Benjamin replied as Lord Stoneleigh came a little further into the room. "Please, tell me about your return to London. Is it for the Season?"

Lord Stoneleigh shook his head.

"I am afraid that I have no particular interest in the latter. I have come to see my solicitors. There are matters that I must discuss with them which could not be put off any longer."

Benjamin poured them both a small brandy and set one down beside Lord Stoneleigh, who had taken a chair in the corner of the room.

"You must try your utmost to sort this matter out. I did not believe that it would be possible at first, but Lord Foster has managed to regain his fortune, and I am already beginning down the path back towards mine. I am *certain* of it, and I say such a thing only to encourage you also."

He waited for the light to grow steadily in Lord Stoneleigh's eyes, but there was none.

"We cannot all have the same good fortune as Lord Foster."

Eager to encourage his friend, Benjamin sat forward in his chair.

"I do not think it good fortune, but rather strength of mind." Picking up his brandy, he took a sip. "It is because of him that I am now quite certain that I will find whoever has taken my fortune from me - although quite how I am to regain it, I cannot yet say!"

"That is assuming you find them in the first place." Lord Stoneleigh shrugged his shoulders. "I come with a specific request, my old friend. It is something that I am ashamed to ask of you, but I have no other choice."

Benjamin sat forward in his chair.

"Of course. What is it?"

"Might I... reside here while I am in London?" Lord Stoneleigh could not seem to look at him. "It will not be for long."

Benjamin spread his hands.

"You may stay with me for as long as you wish. You have no need even to ask! All you need to do is turn up with your things and–"

"That is precisely what I have done." Lord Stoneleigh gave him a small but rather sad smile. "My own townhouse has been let to another upper-class family, who have only just come into their title but have, as yet, no townhouse of their own. Something about their great uncle having sold it some years ago." He waved a hand dismissively. "Regardless, I am now in London without an abode, but I must be here if I am to speak to my solicitor."

"That I quite understand, you must stay with me for as long as you wish, although pray do not think that I am somehow in any better situation than yourself. This is all because of Lord Foster." Picking up his brandy, he shrugged one shoulder. "The man is quite insistent that he will give me whatever he can to aid me in my present circumstances, until I regain my fortune. He is most generous, but I have every intention of paying back every single penny."

A flicker of a smile crossed Lord Stoneleigh's face.

"Mayhap I ought to say the same as you, even though I have very little hope of regaining what is lost."

"But a little is hope enough." Benjamin replied, smiling. "Even a small amount will suffice."

"Perhaps."

Understanding fully the despondency Lord Stoneleigh felt at present, Benjamin chose to leave the conversation at present.

"I will have the footman place your things in one of my guest bedchambers. You are to be as much at home here as you would be in your own townhouse."

At the mention of this, Miss Carshaw immediately came to mind, and Benjamin could not help but smile. He had been rather pleased to surprise the young lady in much the same way she had surprised him when he had found her in his house.

"I am grateful to you for your generosity." Taking a sip of his brandy, Lord Stoneleigh let out a small sigh and closed his eyes. "Tell me then. Have you discovered much?"

"About...?"

"About your lost fortune."

A little surprised that Lord Stoneleigh wished to talk about this once more, Benjamin nodded fervently.

"Yes, a little."

"Tell me what you have discovered"

Benjamin shook his head.

"We were all sent to the East End of London by Lord Gillespie, were we not? I do not know if Lord Foster has informed you, but he is dead."

Lord Stoneleigh did not open his eyes.

"Yes, I am aware. I considered him a friend rather than an acquaintance, so it has been difficult for me to reconcile what he did with the friendship I thought that we shared."

"That I can understand," Benjamin responded carefully. "It seems that Lord Gillespie was responsible for sending gentlemen to the East End and, whilst Lord Montague stole Lord Foster's fortune, he did not steal mine. That was another man entirely – we can be certain of this because of what Lord Montague himself said."

Lord Stoneleigh cracked open one eye.

"What did he say?"

"He would not state much, but what he *did* say was that there are more gentlemen involved in this affair, rather than just himself. Lord Foster believes that there is a situation at present where quite a few gentlemen are involved in a scheme to send other men to those copper hells in the East End of London, with the specific intent to then deprive them of their fortunes using underhanded and utterly dishonorable methods."

Shaking his head, Lord Stoneleigh rubbed at his eyes.

"And how are you ever to find them?"

"Because Lord Foster has provided me with the names of six men closely acquainted with Lord Montague. It seems likely that they are the men who might very well be involved in such a scheme."

"And do you intend to study each and every one of them?"

"That is my intention, yes. Whether I will have any success, I cannot yet say, but it is something at least. To have nothing would leave me quite lost and without even a single shred of hope."

"Much as I find myself at present." Lord Stoneleigh smiled a little sadly. "Well, if I can be of any assistance to you whilst I am in London, please permit me to be so."

"I am grateful to you for your offer. The first gentleman on the list to consider is Lord Drakefield. Do you know much about him?"

"No, I don't. Although..." Lord Stoneleigh's eyes darted from one side of the room to the other as he tapped one hand on his knee. "Is it not so that he has been absent from London this Season? I am certain that he is in mourning for his wife."

Benjamin lifted an eyebrow.

"Is that so? I had not heard. As I have said, I know very little about the man."

"I suppose that you do not need to consider him any further, at least!"

Chuckling wryly, Benjamin gestured to the paper.

"That leaves five others. I suppose I should see whether or not any of them are in London, for if they are not, then I need not even think of them."

"Might I ask who the next gentleman on the list is?"

"Certainly – it is Lord Chambers."

He looked up hopefully towards Lord Stoneleigh, but no flash of recognition came into his expression.

"I do not know that gentleman, so whether he is in

London or not, I could not say. That leaves you with a great deal of difficulty, does it not?"

"But now I have five names instead of six," Benjamin laughed, determined to find some happiness in all of this. "I shall have to begin asking a few more questions. Which means an even greater return to society."

"You have not been attending?"

"I have attended a few events, but never regularly." Benjamin screwed up his features. "They were so very disdainful when I had difficulties with my fortune, but the moment they believed that I had recovered it, they all wished to greet me as warmly as they ever did before. There is a falseness in all of society that I dislike. Besides which," he continued, picking up his brandy, "there are so many young ladies being flung in my direction that I cannot so much as glance at any of them, for fear that their mothers will take that to be a flicker of interest. Can you imagine what would become of me if one of them thought we were soon to become betrothed? They would not know that they had tied themselves to a pauper!"

"That would be difficult indeed," Lord Stoneleigh replied. "Tell me, what occasion do you attend this evening?"

"A simple soiree. Lord Hendrickson has always hosted excellent gatherings in previous years, and mayhap I will be able to discover something about these other gentlemen this evening. I could send word to Lord Hendrickson, as you are present in London, if you wish to join me."

Lord Stoneleigh shook his head, then rubbed one hand over his brow.

"No, thank you. At present I have no eagerness to return to society, but I hope you have a pleasant – and productive – evening."

The drawing room was already full of guests by the time Benjamin arrived. Considering it to be rather good fortune, given that he could wander in and out of the guests in an unobtrusive manner, Benjamin began to do so, seeking to be as inconspicuous as possible. It was a good deal easier to overhear the conversations of the others this way, although the first few he lingered to overhear held nothing of any importance.

Continuing to walk slowly, he kept his mind on the names of the gentleman on the list - five of whom were now of interest, rather than six.

His attempt to not be noticed was not to last long, for one of the disadvantages of his return to society was that people were eager to make certain that he knew just how glad they were to see him again. A young lady and her mother drew near him, and Benjamin was forced to pull his attention away from his own intentions.

"Good evening, Lord Wiltsham. How relieved I am to see you here this evening, for we have been present for some minutes but not yet had anyone to converse with."

"I am glad to be of assistance to you, then." Benjamin forced a smile, having very little recollection of either the older lady or the younger one whom he presumed to be her daughter. If they had been introduced to each other some time ago and, given all that had happened, they would surely have to forgive him for forgetting their names! "Might I be so rude as to beg of you to remind me –"

The elder lady did not appear to be interested in sharing her title or, indeed, listening to anything that Benjamin had to say, for instead, she grasped his arm and drew herself closer, her eyes wide.

"Have you heard the news?" Benjamin, a little perturbed, shook his head and tried to carefully remove his arm from her furious grip, but it was not to be. The lady was beaming up at him, her eyes still searching his. "It is about Lord Chambers!"

"Lord Chambers?" Benjamin, repeated, suddenly astonished to hear the name of the very next gentleman on his list being spoken by this lady. "I have never been introduced to him."

"Have you not?" A quick glance towards her daughter had Benjamin lifting his eyebrows. Evidently, this gentleman was of some importance. Would it be of any help to him? "Well, might I suggest that you must introduce yourself to him immediately, although he is not here this evening, which is something of a disappointment. He is a most *interesting* gentleman, who spends a good number of months over on the continent each year. However, he almost always returns to England for the Season, although he disappointed us last year." Her fingers squeezed his arm. "But this year, he has come back to London with his *wife!*"

Blinking, Benjamin nodded slowly.

"I see."

"His wife!" she exclaimed again, as Benjamin tried to find some sort of astonishment in that statement. "She is from the continent, it is said, and very grand indeed!"

"How extraordinary." Putting as much excitement into his voice as he could muster, Benjamin considered for a moment. "And did you say that he has only just returned from the continent?"

The lady nodded.

"Yes, only last week!"

Benjamin nodded slowly, his heart lifting a little. *If Lord Chambers has been traveling outside England, then he cannot have been involved in Lord Montague's schemes. That is one gentleman less.*

"A gentleman of interest, certainly."

"Indeed," she agreed at once, her voice a little higher with enthusiasm. "I am a little astonished to hear that you have not been introduced to him before now." She frowned, as if she were silently blaming him for his lack of foresight. "You must meet his wife also, of course. They will be the talk of London!"

Which is something of a relief for me.

If the *ton* were busy speaking about Lord Chambers and his new wife, then they were less likely to discuss matters pertaining to his own present situation, or that of his friends. Smiling to himself, he nodded, smiled, and appeared to give great attention to everything that the lady said, as she continued to talk in great detail about the gentleman, ignoring the giggles from her daughter as best he could. Silently, however, he was striking off Lord Chambers' name from his list.

"Did I hear you speak of Lord and Lady Chambers?"

A clear voice caught Benjamin's attention, and he turned his head to see none other than Miss Carshaw coming to join them. Her smile was wide and directed towards the young lady, whose name, as yet, Benjamin could not recall.

"We are, Miss Carshaw!" the older lady said, clearly delighted that someone else understood her interest. "You have heard of him?"

"I certainly have! Who, indeed, has not?"

Laughing merrily, Miss Carshaw tipped her head back slightly as she did so, and Benjamin found himself suddenly admiring the gentle curve of her throat. But the moment he became aware of it, he turned his head away sharply. When had he begun to take note of Miss Carshaw's beauty?

"Can you believe that Lord Wiltsham is not yet introduced to him?"

Miss Carshaw turned her dancing eyes towards him and smiled.

"Goodness, that is a disastrous thing indeed! We must see that you are introduced to Lord Chambers at the very first opportunity."

Benjamin struggled to hide his grin, delighting in the mock teasing which filled her voice – which both of his other companions appeared not to be able to make out. Her eyes twinkled with stars, a bright illumination in a sea of blue and green shadows, and he found himself suddenly lost in them.

"Yes, well, my daughter and I have been acquainted with Lord Chambers for at least a *year*, I believe, for we were introduced to him last Season." The older lady linked arms with her daughter, but kept her gaze towards Benjamin. "I am certain that we shall be introduced to his wife very soon."

"I am sure you shall."

Clearing his throat, Benjamin looked towards Miss Carshaw, hoping they might continue the conversation, only for the other young lady to smile, reach out one hand towards Benjamin and touch his arm for a moment.

"I recall that you danced with me last Season, Lord Wiltsham." She paused, one eyebrow lifting as Benjamin tried to smile. "I believe it was the cotillion."

"I am afraid I cannot quite remember," Benjamin replied, still struggling to recall the young lady's name. "I am certain, however, that you would have danced *very* well."

Miss Carshaw warmed the air with a smile.

"Alas, I have not yet had the pleasure of dancing with Lord Wiltsham. Tell me, Miss Pennington, is he a good dancer?"

The young lady blushed, smiled, and confessed to Miss Carshaw that yes, she thought Lord Wiltsham an excellent dancer. The tightness in Benjamin's chest loosened with relief, knowing now the name of the young lady, at the very least, although he still could not recall the mother's title.

"Look, my dear, there is Lord Stokes! And he is without any company whatsoever – we must go at once!"

Grabbing her daughter's arm, the older lady immediately began to drag her away from Benjamin and Miss Carshaw's conversation, leaving them standing quite alone. Benjamin's mouth fell open in sheer astonishment.

Miss Carshaw giggled.

"I am sorry that your company was not sought after for long, Lord Wiltsham."

"Thankfully, I am not too perturbed, Miss Carshaw." Seeing the mirth in the situation, Benjamin chuckled lightly. "Unless you also intend to leave my company?"

"No, I think I shall stay here for a little while longer."

Her smile softened and Benjamin, much to his surprise, found his heart quickening a little.

"Would you care for a turn about the room?" The question came to his lips before he had even thought to ask it, and he was uncertain why he had said such a thing, but the words were out of his mouth, and he could not take them back. Miss Carshaw's smile slipped, and a hint of red danced its way across her cheeks. Was it simply from the heat in the room? He could not tell. "You have no chaperone this evening?"

Benjamin winced as he realized that he ought not to be

even *suggesting* walking with her alone, unless under the sharp eye of either her chaperone, father, or mother.

Miss Carshaw laughed easily enough.

"You need not be concerned about such a thing, my Lord, not for me. My brother is present, and I am certain that he will be able to watch for me should he wish it."

A slight puckering of his eyebrows came as Benjamin struggled to recollect the title of her brother, but dismissed it quickly enough.

"So long as you are quite certain that I will not be hauled before him to face his demand for an explanation as to why I was walking alone with his sister in the drawing room, then I suppose I can be quite contented."

"I promise that all shall be well."

She accepted his arm and they fell into step together, with Benjamin a little surprised at how much joy was in this moment.

"This soiree is quite crowded, with many more guests than I had expected, I confess."

"Yes, I would quite agree. However, I have heard that Lord Shadsworth often throws occasions such as this, which have far too many guests invited. It seems that such a thing is almost to be expected of the gentleman!" Miss Carshaw smiled up into his face as Benjamin winced. "I have the impression that you would prefer a smaller number rather than a great crowd."

"Yes, Miss Carshaw, I certainly would, yes." He chose not to go into any particular detail as to why that was. "Would you prefer a smaller, more familiar gathering yourself?"

"I always think that a smaller number is preferable. You can have more intimacy that way."

Miss Carshaw held his gaze, and for a moment,

Benjamin was caught by the way that her eyes swirled with various shades of green, edged with blue. Licking his lips, he pulled his gaze away.

"I quite agree."

"Aha, but I believe my reasons would be quite different from your own. It is solely because I boast very few acquaintances and would be ashamed to walk around a drawing room such as this without anyone to speak with."

Her eyes darted to his once more.

"We could not have that." Benjamin smiled back at her. "Be assured, Miss Carshaw, that, if we are ever in a room together and you are seeking someone to converse with, I would be more than happy to do so."

"I shall hold you to that." Miss Carshaw beamed at him, and Benjamin's heart warmed a little. "I must say that you are a very considerate gentleman, Lord Wiltsham, given that I was found in your townhouse without any real explanation as to why I was there."

A twist of guilt knotted his heart.

"I will not hold anything against you, Miss Carshaw. However, I shall say that in my eagerness to remove you from the house, I did not care to hear your explanations, lest in the time it took, someone had come upon us. But I see no need to put any distance between us here, and nothing untoward has come from the situation, has it?"

"Again, that is most considerate." Her arm tightened on his for a moment as she smiled and lifted both shoulders. "I am glad to have your acquaintance, Lord Wiltsham. Miss Lawrence told me that she thinks that you are the very best of gentlemen, aside from Lord Foster, of course, and I believe that her consideration of you is quite correct."

Benjamin's breath caught, and he felt a little surprised

at her compliments, which sent a gentle wave of warmth up into his chest.

"That is very gracious of Miss Lawrence." Struggling to think of what else to say, he cleared his throat quite rapidly. "Alas, I fear that I must take my leave of you, but I can see that Miss Lawrence herself has arrived. I should not wish to leave you without someone to converse with."

Miss Carshaw took a step back from him, her hand sliding from his arm but her smile remaining.

"I thank you, Lord Wiltsham. You are very kind indeed. I shall make my way to Miss Lawrence directly, and I hope that you enjoy the rest of the evening."

"I am certain I shall."

Realizing that all thought about the other gentlemen on Lord Foster's list had left his mind, Benjamin gathered himself for a moment, then turned away from Miss Carshaw. Striding across the room, he quickly made himself known to a group of gentlemen, trying to insert himself into the conversation, even as lingering thoughts of Miss Carshaw continued to run around in his mind. She had distracted him, certainly, but he had found himself saying things that he had never expected. Miss Carshaw was quite correct in her suggestion that it would be expected for a gentleman to put great distance between himself and a young lady who had behaved as she had done. Why then, was he almost eager to be in her company? Why had he offered to take a turn about the room with her?

"For having just been some time in the company of a beautiful young lady, you do appear to be frowning, Lord Wiltsham."

Benjamin allowed himself a slightly wry smile, as one of the gentlemen in the group addressed him.

"I confess that I am deep in thought," he admitted, as one of his acquaintances chuckled.

"No doubt you are wondering whether or not you ought to snare that particular young lady," another one said. "She is very pretty indeed, but her brother is something of a..."

The man's voice trailed off, and a glance ran around the small group of gentlemen, leaving Benjamin feeling as though he were entirely in the dark as to what they had been intending to say.

"I am afraid I have not become acquainted with her brother. If there is something about him that I should know, then pray, inform me of it at once!"

Another acquaintance cleared his throat.

"If you intend to court Miss Carshaw, then yes," came the reply. "As much as I dislike speaking so about other gentlemen, he is the sort of fellow one must be a little wary around."

"And why should that be?"

For what was the second time, an uneasy glance moved from one gentleman to the next, as though they all knew some great secret that Benjamin did not. He could well understand that they did not wish to speak badly of the gentleman, but if there was something of concern, then that was something that Benjamin himself wished to know.

But why should I be so concerned, if I do not care anything for the lady and have no intentions as regards our acquaintance?

"Permit yourself caution. That is all we shall say," another said, prompting nods from many. "The man keeps matters close to his chest and for good reason. There's many an ill thought in his head, I am sure. His character has worsened ever since he has taken on the title."

"I am grateful to you for your consideration in warning

me," Benjamin stated as the other gentlemen in the group nodded sagely. He waited to see if anyone wanted to say anything further or anything more specific, but they did not. "Miss Carshaw is a very lovely young lady. It is a pity that her brother has put so many off furthering their acquaintance with her."

"*I* shall not be one who is so put off."

Speaking with more fervor than he had intended, Benjamin swiftly looked away, suddenly unable to meet the eye of any of the other gentlemen present. He did not know where such determination had come from, but yet it grew within him steadily. That was what Miss Carshaw had said to him on the day he had discovered her, he recalled. She had been afraid of her brother and his schemes.

Her brother intended her to marry a gentleman of his choosing, he remembered suddenly... and he had brushed it off as though it were a small affair, telling both himself and her that any young lady should be glad to be offered the security of marriage. Now, however, given what his acquaintances had said of her brother, genuine concern rose in his heart for the lady. What sort of husband would this fellow choose for his sister? No doubt he would choose someone of similar character to himself, and if his character was not a good one, then what hope was there for Miss Carshaw to have a happy and contented marriage?

Realizing that he did not even know the title of her brother as yet, Benjamin tried to interrupt the conversation.

"Might I ask what is the name of Miss Carshaw's brother? What is his title?"

Unfortunately, the conversation had already turned to something new, and no one was left to answer Benjamin's question. He tried to ask again on two separate occasions, but the gentlemen were far too busy discussing a diamond of the first water – a young lady by the name of Lady Sophia. Their eager discussion about her, and who might be able to steal her hand, was so great that they did not seem to hear Benjamin's question, and thus he was forced to leave it for the present moment

He lapsed into silence, thinking that what was all the more astonishing was his sudden urge to find out more about Miss Carshaw, and the situation her brother had placed her in. That was far more intriguing than any diamond of the first water! Quite what he intended to do about it, he had very little idea, but as yet that was the only thought in his mind - to the point that he had even forgotten about the other gentlemen he was to be considering. Completely ignoring the rest of the conversation, he let thoughts of Miss Carshaw take him away. The lady was most extraordinary, but even now, guilt tore at him for his response to her cry for help on the day that he had discovered her. He ought to have given a little more credence to what she had said of her brother. The situation was a good deal more serious, and deserved more consideration than he had thought - and to his increasing astonishment, Benjamin found his heart eager to do all that he could to help her.

CHAPTER TEN

"You were walking around the drawing room with a gentleman yesterday." Julia shot sharp eyes towards her brother, who immediately came to a sudden stop, taking in the fact that she was now sitting opposite the very same gentleman who had walked with her at the previous day's soiree. "Pardon me."

He did not even apologize nor come to introduce himself but turned at once and exited the room, leaving Julia all the more embarrassed.

"My brother is often a little..." Finding the correct word impossible to choose, she simply shrugged and spread out both hands. "Forgive me, Lord Wiltsham. My brother ought to have stayed and introduced himself to you, given that you are not yet acquainted. I can only apologize that he has not done so."

Lord Wiltsham gave her an easy smile.

"Pray have no concern on my part, my dear lady, I have come to see *you*, not your brother."

A little relieved, Julia's shoulders dropped.

"In fact, I have come with a specific purpose, Miss

Carshaw." Julia's heart burst with a brilliant and furious hope, which she could fought to contain, her tongue suddenly too big for her mouth, rendering her unable to speak in response. Could there be a genuine desire within him to court her? If he was to offer her such a thing, then it would mean that she need not consider other ways of making him her husband, should it come to it... and even that desire was becoming lesser and lesser with each day. "I am come to apologize to you."

Her hope died away.

"Apologize, Lord Wiltsham?"

"Yes, Miss Carshaw. I was speaking with a few gentlemen yesterday and they informed me that your brother may be –" Something seemed to stick in his throat, and he looked away. "May be someone with a few unlikeable traits, although pray forgive me if I am speaking words which you do not wish to hear. I do not intend to harm you."

Julia shook her head, a little surprised at the conversation.

"You are saying nothing I do not know already."

"And I am sorry for that." Lord Wiltsham leaned forward, his hands clasped and his elbows on his knees. "I should have given your words more credence. I do not know what it was you were intending by hiding, but I ought not to have laughed at you. I ought not to have told you that matrimony was something that every young woman should be glad of. I do not think I completely understood what it was you were struggling with, and I certainly should not have spoken so flippantly. I have come to apologize for that, Miss Carshaw."

That is kindness indeed.

Julia opened her mouth to tell Lord Wiltsham that she

was grateful for his apology, only for the door to open and the butler to step inside before she could speak.

"Forgive the interruption. My Lady, the master wishes you to join him in his study at this very moment."

Heat began to pour into Julia's chest.

"I have a guest."

Gesturing to Lord Wiltsham, she lifted an eyebrow as though the butler had any say in what orders her brother had given.

"I am aware, my Lady. But the master was very clear and stated that I was to fetch you at this very moment."

"I can take my leave."

Lord Wiltsham made to rise, but Julia quickly shook her head.

"I am very much enjoying your company. I should not like you to go - that is, if you would be willing to stay and wait for a short while? I am sure that whatever my brother wishes to say to me will not take long, and I can only apologize for the interruption."

Lord Wiltsham nodded and sat back in his chair. Requesting that the butler send up some refreshments for them both, Julia quickly took her leave, hurrying along the hallway with cheeks that were burning with the heat of embarrassment. Whatever was her brother doing?

Making her way to the study, she stepped inside without so much as a knock. Her brother lifted his eyes to her, narrowing them in obvious frustration.

"Julia. You have no respect. I–"

"I could very well state the same of you, brother. You know that I have a gentleman caller. Why do you pull me away from him? What could not possibly wait for a few minutes more?"

Viscount Kingston glared at her and folded his arms across his chest.

"You are to wed Lord Bullfield." Julia's heart clattered in her chest as she stared at her brother, seeing the glint in his eye, and knowing that there was no possible way he could be jesting. Her mouth opened but she could say nothing, her mouth dry as a cold rush swept over her limbs. "You do understand me, do you not? You are to marry Lord Bullfield. This gentleman, whoever he may be, cannot ever become your betrothed – although that is suggesting he may have an interest in you, which I cannot quite bring myself to believe."

Julia forced herself to speak, her voice rasping.

"You cannot. You told me that I was to have a month."

"And you have made so little progress that I have decided to do what is best for you and secure you a husband before it is too late." Her brother flipped his fingers towards the door, dismissing her. "You may return to whoever this gentleman is, but there shall be no further discussion on this matter."

Julia did not move. She could not. Her feet seemed fastened to the floor, her eyes fixed to her brother.

"Lord Bullfield is one of the very worst of gentlemen. I will not wed him. You already know that I will not."

"What is your alternative?" her brother jeered. "You have nothing. You can *have* nothing save for what I give you. Do not give me your excuses nor your threats, for I will not listen to them. Take yourself elsewhere. Cry into this gentleman's arms for all I care."

With another dismissive wave, he turned his head and picked up some papers, evidently unwilling to listen to a single thing she had to say. Tears burning in her eyes, Julia turned and fled, leaving the room and finding herself quite unable to be composed enough to see Lord Wiltsham again. Making her way directly to her bedchamber, she caught the passing maid's hand.

"Please give my apologies to Lord Wiltsham. He is present in the drawing room, awaiting my return. I cannot see him at the moment. Please, you must do this at once, regardless of the orders my brother has given you."

The maid blinked, but to Julia's relief, squeezed her hand lightly and then hurried away, leaving Julia to her thoughts. Opening the door to her bedchamber, she hurried inside and slammed it shut behind her, closing out the world. Sinking down onto the bed, she buried her face in her hands. Why had her brother shown her such cruelty? He had promised her a month, but then he had taken it away, just when she had thought there might be an opportunity for her with Lord Wiltsham. It seemed that he was determined that she should not have any semblance of happiness. Perhaps in seeing that she had a gentleman caller, he had decided to make certain it could never come to fruition.

But what of Lord Wiltsham?

In the back of her mind, there had always been an idea that she would, one way or the other, find herself betrothed to Lord Wiltsham. That had come from consideration of his character, but the more time she had spent with him, the more she now realized that she could never trick him into anything. There was a consideration of him that had not been there before. Even his call upon her today and his apology had touched her heart in a way she had never expected. She could never force him into marriage by trapping him in some manner. So what else could she do to escape from her brother's intentions and Lord Bullfield himself?

Julia rubbed her eyes, trying to think clearly. If she was not to do anything to trap Lord Wiltsham into marriage, then could she not simply ask him? It would be a very forward thing for her to do, but under the circumstances, what choice did she have? They would not be able to marry, however, without her brother's permission. That realization had her eyes squeezing closed, hope fading away, for she could not expect Lord Wiltsham to elope with her! That would cause a scandal and damage his reputation and she could not do that to him.

"I could always make my way from this house as I did before."

Steeling herself, Julia rose from her bed, aware of the shaking in her legs as she moved across the room. Opening one of the drawers, her fingers soon found the bag she had hidden there. Within, it contained the various items which she had taken from her brother when she had left for Lord Wiltsham's townhouse, the items she had thought to use so that she might live in comfort for a few years. As yet she had not returned them – so could she use them – and the plan – again?

It is only the very bare threads of a plan, but it is a plan, nonetheless.

"I will speak to Lord Wiltsham. If he refuses, then I know what I must do."

This decided, Julia set the items back in the bag and pushed the bag deep into her drawer. Thus far, her brother had not noticed the absence of these items, and she did not have any intention of permitting him to become aware of it either. Perhaps it had been good fortune that had not allowed her the opportunity to return them to their proper places as yet.

Wherever she looked, there was darkness. Her heart

was covered in shadow, and even the very air around her seemed oppressive. Julia battled against the mounting despair in her heart as, sinking back down to the bed, she closed her eyes and clasped her hands tightly together.

"I will not marry Lord Bullfield." Her determined whisper brought a little courage to her otherwise fading hopes. "My brother shall not have his way. I will be victorious in the end."

~

The ball had gone on for some time, and Julia had not yet seen Lord Wiltsham. His absence was noticeable, and she found herself wondering whether or not he actually intended to attend the evening, even though she knew that he had an invitation. Her spirits were very low indeed, to the point that even Miss Lawrence had not been able to raise a smile from her. Her friend was currently dancing with Lord Foster, and Julia was battling with the jealousy which came from watching the happiness that was so obviously between them.

"Good evening."

A hand touched her elbow and Julia turned, a swift hope building in her heart, only to see Lord Bullfield reaching out to grasp her hand with his. She jerked back immediately, pulling herself away from him and giving him no flicker of delight at his company.

"Remove yourself from me at once." Her voice was sharp as he reached for her again, a broad smile on his face that told her he had no interest in anything she was saying. "I have no wish to be in your company this evening.'"

"And what would your brother say to that, Miss Carshaw?"

Lord Bullfield chuckled, but it was not a delightful sound, making Julia shudder.

"I think you must believe that I give credit to what my brother says. Allow me to dissuade you of that notion."

Lord Bullfield chuckled again.

"You will not put me off from considering you my bride. Your brother has informed me of your previous attempts to push particular gentlemen away, but I can assure you that, given what your brother is offering me, I have every intention of remaining close to you."

"Even though I have no wish for you to do so?"

She arched one eyebrow, but Lord Bullfield merely shrugged.

"You are not a consideration in this, Miss Carshaw. You are to do as your brother commands."

"He does not demand that I be in company with you this evening," she stated fiercely, pulling her arm away again as he reached for her. "You cannot think that I have any eagerness for being in your company."

"It is not important to me what you think or feel. Whether you wish to be in my company or not, we *shall* be wed." His eyes darkened. "I can make it so that you will have no opportunity to refuse me."

"Leave me!"

Aware that his fingers were once more wrapping around her wrist, Julia pulled herself away as quickly as she could, but Lord Bullfield seemed unwilling to leave her. In fact, he seemed determined to follow her, no matter where she went. His hand continued to reach out to grasp her as Julia hurried away, swerving in between guests until she managed to walk directly into another gentleman. Her fear was growing swiftly, Lord Bullfield's final words wrapping around her heart as she tried to understand what he meant by such a statement.

"I beg your pardon."

Her vision blurred, her breath rasping she tried to sidestep the man she had collided with, suddenly terrified that Lord Bullfield would find her, and pull her away, to the point that she would be utterly disgraced and have no other choice but to marry him. Strong hands grasped her shoulders, and she was forced to look up, only to see Lord Wiltsham looking down at her.

"Miss Carshaw, I have been looking everywhere for you. Are you quite well?"

She shook her head, struggling to breathe through her fear. She could not stay near him, could not be drawn to him, not when she could never be as close to him as she had once hoped.

"Pray excuse me."

His hands dropped as she moved away, only for him to call out after her. He did not leave her to hurry away, however, but came after her, staying close to her as she continued to move.

"Something is wrong, Miss Carshaw. Pray tell me what it is. Is it the same thing that troubled you yesterday? Is that why you were unable to continue our visit?"

Glancing back over her shoulder at him, the fear that Lord Bullfield was still following her continued to grow as she threw up one hand towards Lord Wiltsham.

"Pray do not concern yourself. I am quite well, I assure you."

"I will not believe that."

His fingers touched hers, but she pulled her hand away sharply.

He cannot be the answer to my troubles, not any longer.

It was foolish to ever allow myself to feel anything more than a brief interest.

"My Lord, do not follow me, I beg of you."

Hurrying forward, she darted another glance behind her, but she was not looking for Lord Wiltsham. Glimpsing Lord Bullfield and his cruel smile, she shuddered and hurried on through the crowd, seeing a door and pushing her way through it. Nothing else mattered to her. All she wanted to do, all she *had* to do, was remove herself completely from Lord Bullfield's company, no matter what steps she had to take to do it.

Going forward into a hallway, she turned towards another door. Turning the handle, she made her way into yet another room, closing the door behind her and breathing in the darkness. Her heart hammered furiously as she struggled to catch her breath, doubling over as sobbing gasps broke from her lips.

I cannot marry Lord Bullfield.

Putting one hand to her heart and the other to her stomach, Julia closed her eyes and took in a deep and steadying breath, trying to calm herself. From the look in Lord Bullfield's eyes, she was certain that he would have done *anything* to gain from her what he wanted. If she refused to marry him, then Julia had no doubt that he would do whatever he could to make certain that she had no choice. The way that he had grasped at her arm made her shudder still.

"Miss Carshaw?"

Swinging around, she immediately began to back away, fearful that it was Lord Bullfield, only for Lord Wiltsham's voice to reach her.

"Are you in here? I cannot see anything."

She said nothing, but her quickened breaths broke through the silence. The sounds of his footsteps, followed by a stumble, caught her attention, only for the swipe of a match to illuminate the room a little. A candle was soon lit, and he held it aloft, obviously looking for her.

"Miss Carshaw."

The softness of his voice was a balm to her pain, but she shook her head.

"You need not..." Aware that her voice was shaking, she drew in another breath. "Please, Lord Wiltsham, you must go. You should not be here."

"Something is wrong." His voice was low and determined. "Yesterday you did not return after meeting with your brother and this evening I found you practically running from someone else, although it seems you will not say who it is. What is the matter, Miss Carshaw?"

"Why should you have any concern for me?" Covering her eyes with one hand, she fought not to give in to yet more tears. "I am nothing to you."

There came a brief moment of silence.

"I cannot answer your questions at present, but I certainly have no desire to leave you as you are. I did not pay heed when you first explained to me your difficulties about your brother, and I should like very much to make up for that now."

She did not understand his reasoning, and squeezed her eyes closed.

"Regardless, there is nothing that you can do. Pray, return to the ballroom. I am sure you have many people who would be glad of your company."

Her mortification over being seen in such a state made her head drop low.

"Miss Carshaw." She jumped in surprise at his voice, now closer to her. The light had not moved, but she realized that he had left it on the mantlepiece and was now looking for her. "You are not alone. If there is something troubling you, then I would like to do what I can to aid you. You are right to state that I have no reason to do so, but what if my conscience is enough of an explanation? Would that content you?"

The broken laugh which came from her lips brought her all the more shame.

"There is nothing anyone can do. I shall have to escape from my brother as I have attempted to do before, in the hope that I shall be successful. Perhaps this should be the moment to say goodbye, Lord Wiltsham."

His hand touched hers and she jerked but did not pull it away.

"You cannot mean that. I do not want that."

Nor do I.

"I certainly do mean it, Lord Wiltsham. There is nothing else I can do. I will *not* marry Lord Bullfield."

His fingers squeezed hers.

"That is the gentleman your brother intends you to marry?"

She nodded in the darkness.

"It is."

Her voice was breaking as she tried to pull her fingers from his, but he held on gently.

"You cannot simply run from London. Where would you go? What would you do?"

"I do not know, but I simply cannot stay here and marry Lord Bullfield."

Her voice was breaking again, and she stumbled forward, meaning to make her way past him, only for him to catch her in his arms. They closed around her waist and, despite her overwhelming sorrow and churning emotions, Julia found herself sinking into him. Her head went to rest on his shoulder, and she took in a shaking breath, knowing that these were the last few moments they would ever spend together.

The door suddenly flew open, and a thunderous voice filled the room.

"I thought I saw you following her! Whatever is the meaning of this, Lord Wiltsham? You cannot hide from me, I *know* you are there!"

Squinting in the light, Julia stepped back from Lord Wiltsham, but it was much too late. Lady Steerford glared at them both, framed in the light streaming from the doorway.

Lord Wiltsham slipped one arm around her waist, and drew her forward to the red-faced Lady Steerford. Her mouth opened, but she had nothing to say, looking up at him only to find herself all the more confused at Lord Wiltsham's easy smile.

"You have interrupted what is a very happy moment, Lady Steerford." His voice was filled with a happiness that Julia could not understand. Surely this was a dreadful moment? One where they ought both be stammering for an explanation and thereafter begging Lady Steerford not to see anything that would cause them difficulty. "I have just had Miss Carshaw's agreement that she will accept my proposal and become my wife."

CHAPTER ELEVEN

The urge to flee, to run, to leave his courage behind and return home was so great that it took every ounce of Benjamin's strength just to remain in the ballroom. Miss Carshaw was by his side as many a gentleman and lady came to congratulate them, but every time Benjamin glanced at her, he caught nothing more than a white face and a somewhat pinched expression.

It had not been his intention to say such a thing, nor to declare himself in such a fashion, but when Lady Steerford had walked into the room, there had been nothing else for him to do but that. He had no inkling as to whether or not Miss Carshaw would be pleased with him, or lost in grief. What if she had thoughts of another gentleman whom she considered more preferable? Closing his eyes for a moment, he let out a slow breath. There was nothing that could be done about that now. They were betrothed and soon to wed.

"Whatever is the meaning of this?"

Rather than looking pleased in any way, Miss Carshaw's brother - the gentleman whose title Benjamin was yet to discover - came towards them with an expression of fury. There was no joy in his face, but rather, his brows were pulled together, sending shadows over his eyes, with his mouth a tight line and his jaw working furiously. For whatever reason, it seemed that the fellow had no pleasure in hearing about his sister's betrothal. In contrast, he appeared absolutely enraged.

"A situation has occurred whereby your sister and I now must wed." Benjamin turned sharply, grasping the man by the elbow, and turning him away from the gathering crowd who, no doubt, would have been eager to hear what the fellow had to say. "It was not intentional. I saw her being pursued by another gentleman – one who wore a wicked grin - and went into that room to make certain that she was quite well, only to be discovered by another lady of the *ton*. Thus, being alone with your sister, I had to immediately make a choice and decided to betroth myself to your sister, to make certain that there could be no damage to her reputation."

All too aware of the many eyes which were watching them, Benjamin narrowed his own eyes as the man's face flushed red and hot.

"You had no right to do such a thing." The man jabbed one finger to Benjamin's chest. "She is *my* sister and *my* concern."

"I am all too aware of that, but as you were not present, I had no other choice but to do what I thought was best. Clearly, the assumption that there was something more between myself and Miss Carshaw could have caused great damage to your sister's reputation. Before Lady Steerford could say anything to anyone else, I told the lady your sister had just accepted my proposal. And now, of course, I am under obligation, and we shall wed. I am in no way distressed by the situation, for I find your sister a most pleasant young woman."

The man's eyes darkened, and his chin tilted.

"No. No, this is foolishness! You need not throw your life away on my sister. You need not betroth yourself to her. I am certain that I can arrange this situation carefully so that no harm comes to anyone. I have another gentleman willing to marry her, who might very well be displeased that she is now betrothed. That was something I have specifically arranged since, after all," he continued, chuckling darkly as he shrugged his shoulders, "it is not as though Julia's company is much in demand."

Bristling at his cruelty, Benjamin shook his head.

"I shall not simply stand by and allow your sister to take guilt upon her shoulders, to have her reputation sullied for something that is not her fault" he stated quite firmly. "I have taken on a responsibility, and I fully intend to fulfill it."

Seeing the man open his mouth again, Benjamin quickly shook his head, putting a smile on his face that he did not really feel. Warnings rose up in his mind about being brother-in-law to this man that so many gentlemen stayed away from, but he pushed them away. It was much too late for all of that.

"And so you are betrothed."

Another voice interrupted their conversation, and Benjamin turned quickly away from Miss Carshaw's brother. Nodding fervently, he stretched as wide a smile as he could onto his lips. He was not about to pretend that nothing had happened, nor was he going to separate himself from Miss Carshaw as her brother requested.

"Yes, indeed we are." His smile was warm as he caught

the flash of interest in Miss Pennington's eyes. "I am betrothed to Miss Carshaw."

Upon hearing her name, Miss Carshaw herself turned her head and came towards him, her eyes a little wide. Was that relief in her expression, or was there disappointment?

"It has been a great surprise for the *ton*," Miss Pennington laughed, but Benjamin did not join in; nor did Miss Carshaw.

Her eyes continued to flicker up towards his, as if she were a little uncertain as to how he truly felt about the matter. They had not had any opportunity to talk since the moment when he had declared them betrothed and perhaps, he felt, everything for her, at present, was a little confusing. Interrupting the flow of conversation from Miss Pennington, Benjamin took a breath.

"Thank you, Miss Pennington, for your congratulations, but you will have to forgive me for stepping away. I intend to take my newly betrothed, Miss Carshaw, for a turn about the room, and mayhap thereafter, the waltz."

Miss Carshaw's eyes flashed up to his but, after a moment, much to his relief, she gave him a small smile. When he offered her his arm, she took it at once and he led her away without any further conversation with Miss Pennington.

Silence followed for some minutes as Benjamin walked with Miss Carshaw near the edge of the room, so that they might be a little less surrounded by noise. Miss Carshaw said nothing, and whenever he so much as glanced at her, Benjamin was a little troubled to discover that she was not even looking in his direction. Tension began to flood through him, twisting his stomach left and right, until he could not wait any longer.

"Miss Carshaw." Taking a breath, he looked down at

her. "You must not go through with this if you do not wish to." Her face looked up towards his and Benjamin reached across to pat her arm. "I am not doing it because I am under obligation to do so. I can understand that you might believe that circumstances have forced this, but I find myself glad that the betrothal has taken place – and under the circumstances, I think this is the wisest course of action. I am a gentleman who keeps to my promises, and I would be glad to continue on towards marriage, so long as you are contented to do so."

His stomach dropped when Miss Carshaw shook her head.

"I do not think that my brother will permit this. I believe that he has already given my hand to Lord Bullfield."

After a moment, his heart turned over in his chest, relief flooding him as he drew in a deep breath.

"In that regard, you need have no concern. Your brother has spoken to me already and attempted to encourage me away from you – but I have ignored his request. Besides which, we have been surrounded by well-wishers since our news broke through the ballroom and we cannot step away from it now – and your brother certainly cannot force it. I believe you may consider our betrothal secured."

Benjamin smiled down at her and, after a few moments, Miss Carshaw's expression changed entirely. Her eyes flew wide, swirling with smudges of olive green as her cheeks colored.

"Was he very angry with you?"

"I could not say, but I also do not care. I refused his offer to step away from our betrothal and have instead determined that we shall wed."

Miss Carshaw blinked at him for a few minutes, then wiped the edges of her eyes with one finger.

"This is quite overwhelming," she whispered. "Please believe me when I state that I did not want any of this. I had no idea that you would be forced into matrimony."

"Of course you did not. I know that you did not plan any of this. It was my choice, Miss Carshaw. It is I who ought to be making certain that you are not angry with me!"

Miss Carshaw shook her head.

"I could never be angry about what has taken place, Lord Wiltsham. You do not know what you have saved me from."

"I believe I do." Benjamin gave her a small smile, reaching across with his free hand to touch her fingers lightly as they curled around his arm. "You shall no longer have to marry Lord Bullfield. Is that not so?"

Her hand tightened lightly for a moment or two, her breath catching in a hurried gasp as if she had only just truly recognized what she had been saved from.

"That is true. I *have* been saved from a future with Lord Bullfield, but you have also saved me from the need to run away from London, and from the life that awaited me with him. You have saved me from a life where I did not know what I should do." Her eyes flickered up to his and then darted away again. "That was my intention, you see. I had every thought of leaving London so that I would not have to marry Lord Bullfield, but I had no plan as to where I would go or what I would do thereafter."

"You would have done that? You would have gone to that extent?"

His heart ached for her as she nodded.

"I would have done anything I could think of to make certain that I escaped from my brother. Could you imagine what my life would have been like if I had wed Lord Bullfield?" A slight shudder ran over her frame and Benjamin caught the edge of it as she leaned against him a little more. "It would not even have been worth thinking of."

Benjamin nodded slowly, taking his eyes away from Miss Carshaw as they continued to proceed around the room, albeit at a rather slow pace. The ball was continuing, with people laughing and dancing and smiling and, no doubt, whispering about the fact that a betrothal had been announced without any prior warning of Benjamin and Miss Carshaw's attachment. For his own part, Benjamin did not much care. He was struggling with a sudden rush of guilt that threatened to overtake his entire being. Had he done the right thing? Yes, he had saved her reputation, but she was now to marry a gentleman who had no wealth. She had no awareness of that as yet, of course, but that was the truth. When was he to tell her? Perhaps she *would* have been better leaving London and going out into the world to seek a life for herself, one way or the other, rather than staying to wed a gentleman such as he.

There will be her dowry, of course. That may aid me in the immediate future.

A twist of his heart brought a sudden rush of pain as he thought of what his world would have been like without her in it, had she left London. It grew all the more as he imagined her standing up in church beside Lord Bullfield, pale and sorrowful. No, despite the desperation of his own situation, he was relieved that they were now to wed – he simply had to find a way to tell her of his situation.

Opening his mouth to say something, Benjamin turned his head to glance at her and again noticed the paleness of her cheeks. His mouth snapped shut. This was not the right time for him to tell her anything, given the present circumstances. No doubt she would be most upset if he did so and, given the state of shock that she was already in at present, it would not be wise to make things worse.

"I am quite sure that you will provide me with a happier life than either my brother or Lord Bullfield could ever have done."

Miss Carshaw's soft voice reached his ears and Benjamin smiled at her.

"I have every intention of doing so, Miss Carshaw."

Her free hand reached across to settle on his arm, her fingers pressing into it gently.

"I should be thanking you for what you have done, and I am aware that as yet, I have not done so. I confess I have been a little overwhelmed by surprise and relief, but I should like you to know just how grateful I am to you for promising yourself to me. To know that I will not have to wed that despicable man, nor will I have to leave London and try and make my own way in life, is of such a relief to me that it feels as though I am already beginning to walk down a different path. I have not the same burden as I had before. But I have you to thank for that."

Benjamin's guilt redoubled itself, as he tried to find something to say, some way to explain matters without making her suddenly afraid. He had done precisely what he had promised himself he would not do: he had managed to betroth himself to a lady of quality, but without having the means to care for her.

"I shall be free." Her voice was soft as if she could not quite take in all that had just happened. "From this moment, my brother has not the same hold on me as he had before."

"No, he does not." That much was true at least. "That is

not to say that we shall not have our own difficulties, however."

Miss Carshaw let out a gentle laugh.

"I am fully aware that not every marriage is easy, Lord Wiltsham. But I shall be forever in your debt for what you have saved me from."

Clearing his throat again, Benjamin looked away. Would she still be grateful when she realized that there was no coin? No wealth to speak of? Perhaps he had done her a great evil in taking her as his bride. Regardless of his decision to hold this back from telling her for the present, he found himself speaking quickly, words tumbling out one after the other.

"Miss Carshaw, you must understand that I have some difficulties at present which will continue on into our married life together. That is... what I mean when I say that we shall have our share of problems."

He was bumbling now, managing to confuse himself as well as the lady, for her eyes darted up towards his, rounding gently.

"I understand. Lord Wiltsham. It would be foolish to believe that every marriage goes on to be a perfectly contented one. I understand what it is that you are trying to say."

"No, you do not." Releasing her arm, he swung around to face her. "Perhaps I have made a mistake." Her eyes rounded all the more and Benjamin silently cursed himself for being so foolish. He had not said what he had intended to, nor what he felt, but from the sudden paleness in Miss Carshaw's cheeks, he now saw she believed he regretted his choice. "That is not what I meant," he said aloud, wanting to remove the fear from her eyes. "We are betrothed now, Miss Carshaw, and I will not step aside from you. These difficulties I speak of, they are significant, however. I am afraid that I have brought you into a situation where you will soon despise me for having done so. My life is not all as it appears."

"Might... might you tell me of it?" The quietness of her voice and the widening of her eyes had Benjamin bowing his head.

"I have not intended to hurt you. I consider us betrothed and we will wed, so pray be assured that I will not turn my back on you. However, I also pray that you will not come to regret accepting the situation as it now stands."

"How could I ever regret standing by the side of the gentleman who saved me from a dark fate?"

Miss Carshaw took a small step forward, and even though they were in the middle of the ballroom, let her fingers twine with his. There was a softness in her expression that Benjamin could not help but respond to, as he pushed his other hand through his hair, even as his heart doubled its speed. No longer could he pretend that he felt nothing for the lady. That was precisely why he had found himself in this difficult situation after all, was it not?

"I do not want to injure you. Miss Carshaw."

"You could not do so. I find my heart open to trusting you."

A small sigh escaped him.

"We will face the wrath of your brother for many days. Perhaps even for years."

Miss Carshaw laughed quietly.

"I have very little concern about what Kingston thinks. Now that I am betrothed, he can say nothing."

A sudden shock rushed into Benjamin's soul, and he found himself staring at the lady, his fingers frozen in place as he held her hand in his. Could it be that what he had just heard was true?

Miss Carshaw's laugh faded away as the rest of the noise in the ballroom seemed to dissipate also. Benjamin stared down into her face, seeing the swirling shades of green in her eyes as she looked back at him, clearly confused about why he was responding with such evident shock.

"Is something the matter, Lord Wiltsham?" Benjamin closed his eyes, hiding the sight of her. "Lord Wiltsham." Her voice was a little more urgent now. "Something is wrong. Pray tell me what it is I can do to aid you." He could not immediately speak, the shock of what he had learned still surging through him. "My Lord, I beg you!"

Struggling to speak, he gave a small shake of his head.

"Miss Carshaw." His voice was hoarse and rasping. "Do you mean to say that your brother is Viscount Kingston?"

When he opened his eyes, she was looking up at him, her eyes huge.

"Yes, that is so. Although I do not understand why you appear so shocked. Have you not known that was my brother's title?"

Benjamin shook his head.

"No, I have not."

Miss Carshaw blinked.

"I do not understand how you can be so troubled. Ever since learning of my brother's title, you have gone very pale indeed. Is there something about him which concerns you? Some significance that I should know of?"

Benjamin opened his mouth and then closed it again, uncertain as to what he ought to say. Miss Carshaw's brother being Lord Kingston had left him speechless. How could he tell her? What words could he find to explain? It was not just that he had not known Lord Kingston's title before, but rather that this understanding brought with it a great deal of astonishment as to how close he had been to someone he had been searching for.

Benjamin was struggling with the realization that one of the gentlemen he had been seeking, one of the names on the list given him by Lord Foster, was none other than Lord Kingston himself. The brother of Miss Carshaw, and soon to be his brother-in-law.

CHAPTER TWELVE

"What is it that you think you are doing? Do you really think you can escape me so easily?"

Julia looked up at her brother, keeping her expression mild, but inside her heart was dancing with the sheer joy.

"There is no question about it, brother. I have managed to escape your intentions and your plans for me, and I cannot deny that I am happy that I have done so."

Her brother came forward, his hand raised, but Julia merely looked at him. Even if he did strike her, it would mean very little. There was nothing he could do now. The *ton* were all too aware of the betrothal tonight, and nothing could be done to end it which would not cause scandal. Thus, Julia felt herself quite safe, able to find security in Lord Wiltsham and their plans to marry.

"He will bring you nothing but pain." Her brother stopped short of striking her, but slammed both of his hands on the arms of the chair, his face leaning down towards her as he sneered. "You will be without hope. You will regret this."

"I hardly think that such a threat is going to concern me

now, brother. I am very aware that I would have found myself in a more than difficult situation had I been forced to wed Lord Bullfield. Therefore, I cannot help but be relieved at this, regardless of your displeasure."

"He has nothing." Her brother's snarl was easily ignored. "Lord Bullfield has everything you could possibly want."

"Save for good character, kindness, consideration, and many other things I could list," she responded, ignoring her brother's harsh tones. "I am not as easily taken in as you believe. I know that I have found a better situation with Lord Wiltsham than I would ever have done with Lord Bullfield, so pray, do not think that I would *ever* make my choice over again."

"You are a fool."

Her brother wiggled one finger in her face, but Julia remained exactly as she was, refusing to allow him to cow her. The courage and determination that he had been so eager to drive out of her was once more fully present within her. She had nothing to fear from him now. Soon he would be just a memory, and she would be free to live her life as she so pleased. It was only a matter of time.

"As I have said, you will come to regret it." Evidently frustrated, her brother stepped back. Julia sighed and merely shrugged. His words were not worth listening to at present. "Be warned, there is more to Lord Wiltsham than there appears. Trust me when I tell you that you will both face great difficulties."

Without another word, her brother stalked from the room, leaving Julia to sit alone once more. She had taken some time to fully believe the fact that she was now to wed Lord Wiltsham, and during that time, had found herself weak with relief every time she thought of it. He had saved her from Lord Bullfield *and* from her brother, as well as from a difficult life, had she chosen to run away. Her brother's threats could not take that happiness from her. Try as he might, she would find herself glad that she had found a new happiness with Lord Wiltsham – a happiness that she would never have found with Lord Bullfield.

There had been a strange situation the previous evening when Lord Wiltsham had stopped suddenly short at news of her brother's title. She had been unable to understand that, uncertain of why he had behaved so. Had he really been so shocked? And if he genuinely had been so, then why had her brother's title caused him such difficulty?

It does not matter. It is as I said to him last evening: my heart is eager to trust him, and that is exactly what I shall do.

That thought finished the very moment that the door opened, and it was announced that Lord Wiltsham himself had come to call. The smile which lit Julia's face was immediately followed by warmth spiraling in her chest as he walked into the room. Far too aware that there were a great many emotions in her heart when it came to Lord Wiltsham, Julia found herself flushing a little. Lord Wiltsham could have no notion of what feelings he roused in her, but for the present, she was happy to contain it, to keep it close to her heart, to let it grow and flourish until one day, perhaps, she might be able to tell him of it.

"Lord Wiltsham. I am very glad to see you. In fact, you have just missed my brother."

"Might you then be able to come for a walk with me, Miss Carshaw?"

Lord Wiltsham did not smile but instead, lifted his chin, his arms clasped behind his back.

Her smile began to crack at the edges.

"Yes, of course. I shall fetch my shawl and my maid and be with you shortly."

"The maid shall have to stay quite far behind us, for I cannot have her anywhere near us for fear that she will overhear our conversation. I cannot have anyone else but you listening to what I have to say." A great and tumultuous fear began to close upon her heart, and she swallowed hard, holding his gaze, but seeing him unflinching. He gave no explanation as to what it was that he wished to say to her. Could it be that he would end their betrothal? "Pray, do not fear." A gentleness came into his tone which had not been there before. "I have upset you, and for that I am sorry. There is no cause for you to be alarmed. I am not going to end our betrothal. I have every intention of taking you to the altar, but there is a good deal that you must know still. It would not be fair of me to choose to keep this from you. You must be informed of it all. I would have no secrets between us."

"Very well." Her brother's words came back to her, but she pushed them from her mind. Whatever these things were, Lord Wiltsham clearly was eager for her to know of them. That in itself was a relief. He was showing her the respect that she had the right to expect, being his betrothed. She could have no cause for alarm in that, surely? "Let me fetch my things. I shall not be a moment."

Lord Wiltsham cast what was now a third glance over his shoulder. The maid was walking at some distance, and he appeared to be satisfied that she was well away from him. He cleared his throat, reached across with his free hand, and touched her fingers lightly as they rested on his arm.

"Again, forgive me for frightening you, if that is what I have done. That has not been my intention. None of this has been my intention, in fact."

"Our betrothal was rather surprising, certainly."

Lord Wiltsham looked over at her sharply.

"That is not to say that I regret it. I am glad that we are betrothed, and I am looking forward to our future, such as it may be."

"As am I."

Licking her lips, Julia chose to say nothing more, looking at the path ahead and waiting for him to say something further.

"When I spoke to you last evening, and stated that there would be some difficulties in our marriage, that is because I have an ongoing trouble at present which has not yet been resolved."

"Difficulties?"

Fear began to wrap itself around her shoulders, sending a cold wind through her very bones.

"Yes. Some weeks ago, I was in London with my friends. We had intended to go and play cards somewhere when one of my acquaintances urged us to make our way to the East End of London. Having never been in such places before, my acquaintance assured us that we would have a great deal of success there. We had no reason not to attend and thus, we decided to make our way there and enjoy the evening." *Is he trying to tell me that he enjoys a little gambling? That would not be at all surprising.* "The following day it was discovered that all six of us had lost our fortunes. Not by our own foolishness, but through the malicious actions of others."

This was spoken with such a matter-of-fact tone that it took Julia a moment to understand what he was saying. Her eyes widened and she stared straight ahead, trying to understand what it was that he was expressing to her. Their steps slowed as he glanced in her direction, his face slowly turning a deep shade of red.

"You... you have no wealth?"

"That is so." Coughing, he shook his head, his cheeks still flushed. "My friend Lord Foster was one of the gentlemen who lost their fortunes alongside me. However, he has managed to recover it, which gives me a little hope also."

Something cold wrapped around her heart as she closed her eyes, suddenly unable to walk alongside him any longer.

"You mean to say that I am marrying a man who has not a penny to his name?"

Lord Wiltsham stopped, turning slightly.

"Yes, that is so. However, I would like to inform you that I have every intention of pursuing matters so that I can regain my fortune."

Julia closed her eyes. Her heart was beating so loudly that she was certain the sound filled the air around them. Her fingers were grasping his arm as she fought to catch her breath.

"If you would allow me to explain?"

Julia drew in a ragged breath, fully aware of weakness threading through her veins.

"I had no intention of attaching myself to anyone, not until I had recovered my fortune. However, under the circumstances, I had no choice but to betroth myself to you. You may find that deeply upsetting, and indeed you may be angry with me for doing so, but my feelings would not permit me to step aside and allow you to be sent forward into a life where you would find nothing but misery."

"Your... your feelings?"

It was as though someone had spun her around so many times that everything was now a blur of color and sound, and she was unable to distinguish one from the other. A loud buzzing came into her ears as Lord Wiltsham cleared his throat and turned away, her arm falling from his.

"That is not the important point at present. When it comes to my fortune, the other gentlemen and I have learned that it was a planned, coordinated attempt by a small number of gentlemen who were eager to steal the fortunes of those who made their way to that particular area of the East End."

Julia shut out the sight of him again, finding herself able to think a little more clearly when she was not looking at him.

"I do not understand." Dropping her head forward, she pressed one hand over her forehead, sliding her fingers down over the bridge of her nose as she took another breath. "This was something done purposefully to you?"

"Yes, we believe so. As I have said, Lord Foster managed to regain his fortune and bring justice to the man who had stolen it from him. I have every intention of doing the same – all I require is a little more time. I have made some progress already."

Julia opened her eyes again, dropped her hands to her sides and sucked in another long breath.

"I can understand why you did not tell me."

"I had no reason to tell you until the point when we became betrothed, since there was nothing of importance between us. We were only acquaintances – until the moment that Lady Steerford came into the room."

Julia caught the quirk of his lips, but also the silver flashes in his hazel eyes as he searched her face.

"I understand that, Lord Wiltsham."

"Pray believe me, I would never have tied myself to you without making certain that we had a prosperous future ahead of us. Circumstances were such that we had no other choice."

Julia nodded slowly and then reached out to take his arm again, catching the slump of his shoulders and the rush of air which broke from his lips, evidencing the relief that he felt at present.

"Given that I had every intention of leaving London with very little to my name, I suppose that I can accept the fact that, for the present, we will be without a great deal of coin."

"You cannot know how glad I am to hear you say such a thing. I have been struggling with this since the moment we became betrothed."

"I should like to hear the entire story, with as much detail as you can provide." Inwardly, she was still shaking, but Julia was determined that nothing would detract from her present relief at being freed from Lord Bullfield. "You state that this was purposefully done. How can you not know who it was that stole it from you then?"

"Because I, as did many of the other gentlemen, found myself with a loss of memory – although I have regained a little of it since. Lord Foster recalled that he was given a brandy which tasted a little strange – and this is what he accounts as what took his senses from him – it had been adulterated with some substance to render him incapable. Whilst I remember very little of that evening, I am certain that the very same thing happened to me."

"That would be most despicable." A frown pulled at her forehead. "How, then, have you any chance of discovering who did such a thing to you, if you cannot remember a single thing about the night when it took place?"

Lord Wiltsham's brow furrowed and for a long moment, he did not so much as glance in her direction. His jaw tightened, and Julia caught her breath, wondering if there was more that he had to tell her. Was he about to take away any further hope that he would one day be able to recover the situation? She pressed his arm.

"You need not be afraid of telling me anything. I am aware that this is already a difficult circumstance and yet I am not pulling away from you, am I? Yes, the situation will be difficult, but I am all too aware of just how fortunate I am to be betrothed to you."

Lord Wiltsham shot her a glance under a slightly lifted eyebrow.

"You truly believe such a thing? I have just told you that we have no fortune, no prosperity, and no comfort for the future."

"But yet I see that I am safe from a life where I would have been ignored, torn down, rejected and no doubt injured by Lord Bullfield. Instead, I am to marry a gentleman who has a kind heart, who is respectful and considerate and who offers me more than Lord Bullfield ever could." The softening of his eyes made her smile. "Have no doubt, Lord Wiltsham, I am all too grateful for the great happiness that will be mine in being your wife. Whether or not we have any significant fortune, I will always be glad that I can count you as my husband, remembering what it is that I have been kept from." Speaking with great sincerity, she smiled up into his eyes. "The future you offer me is far better than the one I would have had with Lord Bullfield, or from my brother's hand. I am not only glad that you have been able to share this with me, but I am also relieved, for now we can step into the future together, knowing precisely what it is that is before us, and going into it together. There will be no fear or doubt, but only a determination that we shall cling together, regardless of the circumstances."

Lord Wiltsham smiled, but it was only brief, and gone at the very next moment.

"And yet, there is more still."

"Tell me."

His lips worked and he shook his head.

"I am afraid of what it will do to you, Miss Carshaw. I care for you and would not see you injured."

A knot formed in her chest, her chin lifting as she looked into his eyes.

"You have heard all that I have spoken to you, have you not? I want to know all, so that we might go into our future as one. Pray, do not keep anything from me. I promise you, I am prepared."

Lord Wiltsham looked back at her, then turned his head away as they meandered slowly through the gate into Hyde Park.

"What if I was to tell you that your brother is one of the gentlemen whom I am presently considering to most likely have been involved in this wicked scheme."

Julia came to an immediate stop, her legs refusing to continue moving. When she turned to face him, Lord Wiltsham was nodding slowly, as if in confirmation of what she presently feared.

"How... it cannot be!"

Her breathless voice did not seem to belong to her, a cold hand grasping around her heart as she struggled to breathe.

"Again, I have shocked you, but you are right, I could not have kept this from you. That is why I responded in the way I did last evening, when you told me your brother's title. It came as a genuine shock to me, for he is one of the gentlemen that I have been considering as responsible for the loss of my fortune."

"I still do not understand."

Julia blinked rapidly, wondering if everything else would fade away if she continued to simply stare up at Lord Wiltsham. Perhaps he would shake his head, telling her that he was sure he was mistaken but instead, he simply held her gaze and smiled sadly.

"You may turn away from me if you wish, my dear. I would not hold it against you, but I must tell you the truth. Lord Foster has given me a list of men who were close to Lord Montague, the man who stole his fortune from him, and who we believe was at the heart of it all. He is gone to the continent now, so there is nothing further we can learn from him."

"But..." Closing her eyes, Julia swallowed hard. "This list...it contains my brother's name?"

"It does. There were only six names present. One only returned to England a few days ago, so would not have been able to have been involved. Another is at home mourning the loss of his wife."

"Then there are three others, are there not?" Rasping, her hand clung to his arm. "It does not mean that my brother –"

"No, indeed it does *not* mean that your brother is responsible. Not as yet. But I have been considering the matter and I have wondered if there was any reason for him to be so eager to push me away from you. Might I ask you what happened the day that I came to call? Why did you not return? Was that the point when he told you that you were to wed Lord Bullfield?"

Julia's throat constricted and she dashed one hand over her eyes.

"Yes, that was the very moment he did so." The truth burned in her throat, but she did not stop herself from speaking it. "Yes, that is exactly what happened."

"When he came into the drawing room and saw me present, mayhap it was then that he realized I had an interest in courting you - and then he made certain that it could not be so."

"Perhaps." Struggling to find another explanation, Julia squeezed her eyes tightly shut. "But perhaps it is that he only wanted Lord Bullfield to wed me for his own purposes, rather than simply pulling me away from you."

Lord Wiltsham nodded, as she opened her eyes to look up at him.

"Yes, it may be so. I will not pretend that such a thing is not a possibility. As I have said, I have no proof, as yet, that your brother is in any way involved in the scheme, save for the list that Lord Foster had has given me."

Julia turned her head away, battling against the tears in her eyes.

"I do not know why I am so eager to defend him." Shrugging her shoulders, she let them fall heavily. "He has not shown me any kindness. Indeed, he has been nothing but cruel to me these last few months."

"There will always be an eagerness to defend one's family. I understand that, and I would not lay any blame upon his shoulders until I have absolute proof. I want you to be aware, however, that there is a possibility. And that possibility is that your brother is involved in a scheme whereby he steals the fortunes of other gentlemen."

"But that doesn't make any particular sense. He has his own fortune, and is going to great lengths to protect that from me, and my requirements upon it. Why then, should he desire more?"

Lord Wiltsham shook his head.

"I cannot answer that. If your brother is already a rich gentleman, it does bring to mind the question as to why he would desire yet more wealth - but could it not also be said that the rich man is always eager for more riches?"

Julia dropped her head, battling against the urge to break down into furious tears. There was truth in what Lord Wiltsham said, loath as she was to admit it.

"That is precisely what my brother is doing, Lord Wiltsham. In forcing me to wed, he is making certain that any coin he has can be kept solely for himself."

"That is the reason he gave for forcing you into marriage?"

She lifted her head and held his gaze.

"Ever since he has taken on the title, I have seen his character change. There is not one shred of kindness in him, for he thinks only of himself. Indeed, he went as far as to declare that my father was foolish in blessing my mother with gifts of love and affection. Those words have brought great injury to my heart, and shown me that my brother is not the man I once knew him to be." A lump lodged itself in her throat, but she continued, for, if she could not speak honestly to her betrothed, then who could she speak to? "Therefore, after only a few minutes of consideration, I must admit that there is every possibility that my brother is involved in this affair. As much as I would like to state that there is no possible reason, no possible way, for him to have done anything of this sort, my heart states entirely the opposite."

Benjamin pressed her hand, his eyes glowing gently with a sympathy and tenderness that sought to bind up her broken heart. That gave her great comfort, and she used that comfort to build courage in her heart again.

"I have left you with a great burden." He moved a little closer, not looking at her, but the space between them. "If I could, I would enfold you in my arms at this very moment. I would hold you close and tell you that I care for you deeply and that I am sorry for the pain I am bringing to you."

She shook her head.

"It is not you who has brought this pain, Lord Wiltsham. That is my brother. Your honesty in telling me all of this is something I greatly value."

"I am only sorry that you are marrying a gentleman with very little coin."

The heavy sigh which followed had her frowning.

"I do not understand that entirely. If you have no money to speak of, how can you live in a manner which indicates otherwise?" A sudden realization dawned on her, and she continued speaking, just as his mouth opened in explanation. "There are no improvements, is that not so? It was an excuse only, so that you might reside with Lord Foster for a time."

He nodded.

"I have very generous friends. Lord Foster recovered his fortune, and has insisted that he use some of it to make sure that I regained a little comfort. In the week after the theft, I returned to my country estate. My man of business informed me that I had only a few weeks left before I was forced to encourage my staff to find other employment – and thus I removed them from my London townhouse, simply because I could not afford them. It is only Lord Foster's generosity that has returned me to this position. The *ton,* you see, believe that I am fully recovered, perhaps thinking that there actually was no loss of fortune, merely improvements being made to my townhouse. When I am successful in regaining what is lost, then I have every intention of giving back every single penny to Lord Foster that he has put towards my comfort."

"You sound a little more hopeful that you will be able to do such a thing." She smiled up at him despite the ongoing troubles of her heart. "I fully believe every word you have told me, Wiltsham. You are a man I *know* I can trust. Why would I think that you would choose to lie rather than speak the truth in this matter?"

Lord Wiltsham smiled at her, his hazel eyes light.

"You are the most extraordinary creature," he confessed to her, making a blush color her cheeks. "I do not know how I shall go about proving whether or not your brother is the one responsible, but I shall give every thought to achieving it so that we might know the truth as soon as possible. I should like to spare you as much distress as I can."

"You have already spared me from a great deal of distress." Her heart warmed as his gloved hand lifted to brush down her cheek, ignoring those who were walking through the park near them. "And now we find ourselves here. I am certain that there will be happiness between us, regardless of what we achieve concerning your fortune – and it will be a happiness that I would never have found elsewhere. That will be enough for me, Wiltsham. That will be more than enough."

CHAPTER THIRTEEN

"I have informed her." Benjamin looked from Lord Foster to Lord Stoneleigh and back again. "Thankfully, she understands and accepts everything."

Lord Foster nodded.

"And here I was, thinking that you hadn't wanted to consider *any* young lady at this present moment. I am quite certain that you told me that you would not do so until you had regained your fortune."

Benjamin grimaced.

"Perhaps I was foolish in following her that evening, but I could not ignore the fact that she was clearly in great distress, and from one look over my shoulder I could tell that she was fleeing from one particular fellow who had a wicked grin as his eyes followed her. I feared what would happen to her if I left her alone."

Lord Stoneleigh and Lord Foster shared a glance, only for Lord Stoneleigh to grin broadly.

"I think I am very happy for you, despite the strange circumstances."

"I appreciate your congratulations, although I am not

filled with happiness. When I first informed Miss Carshaw about my lack of fortune and, thereafter, about my concerns over her brother, there was a great deal of upset caused by my words."

Lord Foster shook his head.

"That is understandable, but it is good that you told her the truth."

Letting out a snort, Benjamin scowled.

"You cannot know the astonishment and the distress that came into my heart when I discovered the title of her brother. Quite how I went for so long without being informed of it, I do not know. Perhaps things would have changed had I heard it beforehand."

"You should be *glad* that you did not know, given that you would have missed out on what is clearly going to be a situation of happiness since you have a growing care and concern for the lady – and she seems contented to stand by your side," Lord Foster put in. "What are your intentions now? How you intend to prove that Lord Kingston either is, or is not, involved?"

Benjamin's scowl darkened all the more.

"I have considered it, but I fear I must ask Miss Carshaw if she would be willing to aid me." The thought twisted his stomach. "It is not something I am eager to do, given the struggle she has already faced, but I believe it is something I must do. Lord Montague has gone from England so I cannot speak to him, although I would dearly love to do so."

"Yes, last I heard, he was on the continent," Lord Foster rolled his eyes. "Exactly how long he intends to stay there, I cannot imagine, although I confess that I do not find myself sorry over the possibility that he might remain there for many years yet."

"Nor indeed do I, despite the circumstances," Benjamin had to agree. "It is better for him to remain far from society. Therefore, my only choice at present is to make my way to Lord Kingston's home, and into his study, which will require Miss Carshaw's aid."

"Into his study?" Lord Stoneleigh repeated, as Benjamin nodded slowly. "You intend to look for evidence there, I presume."

"Yes. I must find a way to prove that he is the man who has taken my fortune. I find myself believing, after further consideration, that he is responsible. After all, what other reason could there be for him to try to drive me far from his sister, if it were not that he did not want her to wed the man he had robbed - for fear that he would be discovered."

"Mayhap because he wanted her to wed Lord Bullfield. There must be something between them for the man to agree to such a thing."

"Then why not insist upon that at the very beginning? Miss Carshaw stated that her brother initially gave her one month to find and secure her own husband."

"Perhaps because he believed that she would be entirely unsuccessful, and wanted to use the opportunity to prove to her the strength of his hold upon her life. After all, you have been told by many a gentleman that Lord Kingston is a man to be avoided, have you not?"

"Yes, that is so, but that still gives Miss Carshaw the chance to be successful. If he only ever had intended for her to wed Lord Bullfield, I do not think that he would even have allowed the possibility of her success," Benjamin argued.

"I can understand your point of view. You must be careful, for, as I have said, Lord Kingston is not a man to be trifled with. If you have forced his hand by determining that you will wed his sister when he had other plans already in place, then you will have angered him."

"I care not." Benjamin stated, firmly. "My only consideration is for Miss Carshaw. I want to make certain that she is free from her brother and if possible, I wish to provide her a life where she is comfortable and contented." A smile lifted his lips as he considered what she had said previously. "She insists that she can be more than happy without my wealth, but I am certain that it would be a great deal of help to us both if I were to recover my fortune."

"I am certain it would be also," Lord Foster agreed wholeheartedly. "Let me also suggest another thing that you might wish to use. It may be a less intrusive way of discovering whether or not the man is involved."

"Yes?"

Lord Foster considered for a moment, looking away as one hand rubbed under his chin.

"You state that the man your fortune went to was identified in that contract as a gentleman by the name of Baron March."

"That is the name my solicitors were given, yes. But there is no such fellow."

"Then why not use that name in front of the Viscount? Study his reaction. If he responds in a manner that tells you he knows the name, then you can be more certain of his involvement. If he does not so much as blink, then perhaps you are on the wrong trail."

"You could also ask Miss Carshaw to speak it rather than yourself," Lord Stoneleigh suggested. "If she is willing, that is. It may come as more of a surprise from her whereas he might be more on his guard when it comes to you."

"A wise suggestion indeed, gentlemen." Benjamin considered for a moment. Would Miss Carshaw be willing to do such a thing? She had tried to defend her brother once already, but he understood her reasons for that. It had been shock speaking, rather than outright denial. If she wanted to know the truth, then would this not be a way to discover it?

"I will speak to Miss Carshaw. If she is willing, then that is what we shall do. If not, then I shall speak to Lord Kingston myself," he declared, as both gentlemen nodded. "As you are both no doubt aware, the lady means a great deal to me. I do not wish to cause her any distress. If I can spare her from it, then I will."

"Speak with your betrothed," Lord Foster suggested. "If she can do this, then it will bring you both a great deal of clarity, which, at this moment, is all that you require."

Benjamin nodded, then watched as Lord Stoneleigh rose from his chair, making his way across the room. Pouring a brandy, he handed it to Lord Foster and then poured a second, which he gave to Benjamin himself. The third he kept, standing in the center of the room, and lifting it in a toast.

"Through all of these difficulties, you have found a happiness with Miss Carshaw that we both pray will bring you a great deal of contentment in the years to come. Whether these difficulties are ever resolved or not, might you both step into your future with joy in your heart that no circumstances can tear from you. May you be as one together, moving along the path of your lives and building a bond so strong that none will be able to break it."

Benjamin smiled and thought of Miss Carshaw. From the very strange moment when he had found her in his house, there had grown something so very strong between them that he could not bear to think of ever parting from her. It was everything that Lord Stoneleigh had said, and Benjamin recognized himself fortunate that he had gained something so wonderful in the midst of what was a great struggle.

"To Lord Wiltsham and Miss Carshaw."

Lord Foster grinned, lifted his glass, and took a long sip, just as Lord Stoneleigh did the same. Benjamin lifted his glass aloft for a moment longer, looking at the amber liquid and smiling softly to himself as his heart filled with a great and overwhelming love for the young lady.

"To the incomparable Miss Carshaw," he murmured, before draining the glass.

∼

It was strange how much his heart shot upwards when he caught sight of Miss Carshaw. She was not even looking at him, and yet he found himself inexplicably excited to be in her company once more. He took her in, his gaze going from the crown of dark hair to the way her fingers curled up into her palms when she caught his gaze. His eyes went to hers and he smiled, waiting until her lips curled back in response.

I do not like having to ask her about her brother.

Making his way towards her, he smiled and reached out with one hand. She took it quickly enough, but then dropped it, and curtsied instead.

"Good evening, Lord Wiltsham."

A quick shift of her eyes to her left told Benjamin that her brother was nearby and, of course, would be expecting nothing but decorum. Given all that he had still to discover about the fellow, Benjamin did not wish to cause any difficulties or make more of an enemy of him than he already had.

Bowing, he gave her a warm smile.

"I am very glad to see you. You look well. I am glad of that."

"I am *very* well, I assure you."

Benjamin assumed that this was said so that he might be encouraged that what they had spoken of, with regard to her brother, had not caused her any prolonged distress. His shoulders relaxed as a relief he had not known he required spread through his chest, warming him.

"I am very well aware, Miss Carshaw, that as yet we have never stepped out together to the dance floor. I do hope this evening that you would be willing to dance with me."

Her bright smile was enough of an answer.

"I should be very glad to, Lord Wiltsham."

"Excellent. And what is more, no one will think anything of it if I steal more than one dance from you."

A light flush licked her cheeks.

"I cannot think of anything I would want more than to spend the entirety of the evening in your company."

"I am glad to hear it. There are some things I should like to speak with you about, but perhaps this evening is not the right moment."

Miss Carshaw shook her head.

"No, I think some things take greater precedence than the mere joy of an evening, do you not? I should be happy to talk with you about whatever it is you wish to discuss."

"I am glad of that. Your willingness is greatly appreciated, particularly when I know this is a difficult conversation."

"But one that I am altogether grateful to you for being willing to have with me," came the reply. Music had begun and Miss Carshaw's face lit up. "Perhaps we might consider stepping out together now, Lord Wiltsham? It would mean that we could speak a little more openly."

This last sentence was said in a low tone and Benjamin glanced over his shoulder to see none other than Lord Kingston glaring at him.

"Perhaps in a moment." Recalling his friend's advice that he ought to maintain as civil an acquaintance with Lord Kingston as possible, Benjamin stepped away from his betrothed for a moment. "Good evening, Lord Kingston." He spoke as pleasantly as he could, but the gentleman glowered at him. There was a darkness in his expression which could not be mistaken for anything else - it was clear that Lord Kingston severely disliked Benjamin, and the malice in his eyes was not something that he could easily ignore. Clearing his throat, he did his best to maintain a civil expression. "I am aware that we have not made the best of introductions. No doubt you are a little frustrated at what has taken place between your sister and I, given your plans for her, but I can assure you that there is a great deal of admiration and respect in my heart for her. I have every intention of making certain that she is well cared for."

"Is that so?"

The thin line which slashed across Lord Kingston's mouth sent Benjamin's heart quickening. Lord Kingston's disdain was obvious, but as yet there was no particular reason for it, other than the belief that Benjamin had done something untoward as regarded his betrothal to the lady.

"Yes, that is quite so. It is my singular determination, in fact."

Lord Kingston lifted an eyebrow.

"And how exactly do you plan on doing such a thing? Poverty is your friend at present, is it not?"

Benjamin blinked, looking back at Lord Kingston for a

long moment without saying a single word, and it was not until some seconds had passed that Lord Kingston cleared his throat and looked away. Had he realized what a mistake he had just made?

"I must beg to understand what you mean by such a thing, Lord Kingston." Keeping his voice as steady as possible, Benjamin tilted his head to one side. "If there are any rumors about my present circumstances, I would be grateful to you if you would inform me of them."

Lord Kingston cleared his throat and shook his head.

"I only mean to state that I must be certain that you are able to care for my sister."

"But that is not what you have asked me."

Benjamin was not about to let the fellow weasel his way out of what had been said. To his mind, this now declared quite certainly that there was motivation behind Lord Kingston's attempts to remove his sister from Benjamin's arm. Yes, there had been some rumors about his lack of fortune, but the *ton* now believed that he had been restored, given that he was able to return to his townhouse and drive his carriage about town just as he had done before. Would Lord Kingston truly have made such a remark if he had not been quite certain that things were not as they appeared?

Lord Kingston coughed harshly, his eyes sliding back towards Benjamin.

"Surely you must understand a gentleman's concern for his sister?" he declared, looking back at Benjamin with a sharp eye, as though daring him to disagree. "I only meant to suggest that you may find yourself without coin in the future and wondered what it was you intended to do, if such a situation came about."

"I see." Benjamin did not believe this in the least, but he could not say so, given the current situation. He did not want to put Lord Kingston on his guard. "Then let us hope that we might become better acquainted in the months and years to come so that I can prove to you that your sister will have a long and contented life by my side. I shall treat her with as much consideration and as much kindness as I can. Despite the strange nature of our betrothal, I find myself a very happy man indeed."

Lord Kingston muttered something and looked away. After a few seconds of silence, he returned his gaze to Benjamin.

"Very good." He did not say that he was happy for his sister, nor that he accepted anything that Benjamin had said, but it was a clear enough dismissal that Benjamin took without upset. Turning away he made his way back to where his betrothed was waiting, seeing the anxiety in her bright eyes. "My dear, you need not worry." He pressed her hand, and she smiled at him, but it did not send any relief into her gaze. "Your brother has said nothing to perturb me. In fact, there was something of a confirmation of my suspicions in what he said, but I shall not explain at present. Come now. The cotillion is about to begin. Should you like to dance it with me?"

This time, a gentle chuckle escaped from Miss Carshaw's lips.

"Yes, I believe I should like it very much. Given that Miss Pennington believed that you were an excellent dancer, it would be a pity not to discover such a thing for myself."

Benjamin laughed quietly.

"It would be, certainly - and as we dance, perhaps I can speak with you about the plan I have at present."

She took his arm, and together they walked out towards the middle of the ballroom, where couples were forming up for the dance.

"A plan?"

"Yes, my dear. A plan to discover the truth about your brother. It may require something of you, but if you do not feel able, then I shall not press you to take part."

Miss Carshaw shook her head.

"No. Whatever it is that you intend to do, know that I will stand by you and assist however I can. If my brother has been involved in this, then I should like to assist in you recovering your fortune from him. And if he has not done so, then at least I shall have relief, knowing that he has not behaved in such a wicked manner."

"Only if you are certain, my dear Julia. I do not wish to cause you any extra difficulty when the situation is as strained as it is at present."

She stepped away so that there was a space between them as she curtsied and he bowed, ready for the dance to begin.

"Your care and consideration of me is greatly valued, Lord Wiltsham, but I assure you that my loyalty is now to you, rather than to my brother. Whatever is required of me, I will do it without hesitation. Just say the word and it shall be done."

Benjamin took her hand and found himself awed by the strength of the woman before him.

"You are the most incredible creature, Julia," he told her, seeing the blush rise in her cheeks. "For all that our betrothal has been a strange one, I find myself becoming more grateful for it every day. Your courage is extraordinary. I speak the truth when I state that I am overawed by you. I think I shall spend every waking moment of the rest of my days reminding myself just how much I have gained in taking you as my bride."

Miss Carshaw's blush grew still, but she continued smiling.

"I feel much the same, Lord Wiltsham. We are together now, are we not? We are one together, and in that, I stand with you in whatever troubles and difficulties may come our way." Her hand released his. "Now tell me of your plan."

CHAPTER FOURTEEN

Taking a calming breath, Julia tugged aside the lace curtain and glanced out of her window, seeing her brother's carriage pull away.

Yes, she could now send a note to Lord Wiltsham to inform him that her brother was gone from the house as he had requested, but what difference would that make to their present situation? During the ball yesterday, Lord Wiltsham had informed her about everything which was required so that they could find out, one way or the other, whether her brother was involved with this dreadful scheme. He had told her about 'Baron March' and had suggested that there might be a document of some sort in her brother's study which could link him to that particular name. His thought had been that, if her brother left the house, she could send him a note, which would then state that there was an opportunity for him to make his way to the house and search through Lord Kingston's study, although certainly not written in so direct a manner as that, lest anyone unintended discover it!

But why could *she* not do so? After all, it would save

them a good deal of time and also, if her brother were to return unexpectedly, she could quickly make her way from the study without him ever being aware of her presence there. If Lord Wiltsham was present, then would not it be that he might become suspicious?

She had to hope that the staff would not inform her brother that she had been in his study if she was seen. Many of them were helpful and polite to her, but that did not mean that they gave her their loyalty. On the whole, however, she had found the servants kind and prayed now that such a kindness would continue, should she be spotted. All the same, she found herself rather afraid as she hurried along the hallway towards the study. What would she find there? If she discovered something which linked her brother to Lord Wiltsham's lost fortune, then what exactly were they to do next? Show him the evidence and demand that he return the funds? He could simply refuse.

Lord Wiltsham will know what to do.

There were no footmen or maids nearby as she reached her brother's study door. Turning the handle, she stepped inside carefully, wincing at the creak which came from the old door. Closing it behind her, she pressed her back against it, looking around as her heart drummed furiously. Her eyes widened as she took in all the drawers and bookshelves which covered the walls of the room, pushing her into the center of it. What exactly was she meant to do? Where was she meant to begin?

Anything he had as regarded that dreadful scheme, surely he would wish to hide it.

Stepping away from the door. Julia took in a deep breath. Her hands were shaking as she lifted the first few papers from her brother's desk.

I have no need to be afraid. He is not even home.

There was nothing immediately to hand which would link him to Lord Wiltsham and the situation he now found himself in. Looking about her, Julia struggled to know where to look next. With very little idea as to how much time had passed, she searched through various papers, but nothing came up that had any inscription of the Baron's name upon it.

Letting out a hiss of breath, Julia ran one hand over her forehead. This was useless.

A sudden knock at the door had her yelping in surprise as she jumped back, her hand going to her heart as she fought not to make a single sound. The door slowly opened without warning, and she staggered back suddenly, desperately afraid that her brother had returned - although why he would knock made very little sense.

"My Lady."

Much to Julia's surprise, the butler stepped inside. A jolt of fear had her staggering forward.

"I know I ought not to be in here. Pray, do not tell my brother. It is only that –"

"My Lady. I do not wish to concern you, but your brother will return soon. He stated that he would not be gone for long."

Julia closed her eyes, hot tears burning against her lashes. The butler was doing what he could to protect her and, despite her failure, she was grateful for that.

"I see."

"Might I ask what it is that you are searching for?"

Julia shook her head.

"I... It does not matter. I do not think that I have any hope of finding it."

The butler nodded but did not move.

"My Lady, most of the staff here have always been

concerned for you – although I would warn you to be cautious around some of the newly hired maids and footmen." Spreading his hands, he spoke with great frankness. "The master has slowly been replacing each of the servants in this house and I am certain that he will, one day soon, wish to remove me also. If such a thing occurs, might I beg of your assistance in finding new employment?"

A single tear dropped to Julia's cheek.

"Yes, of course. You know that I am to wed, I am sure. But my husband to be and I would be more than willing to do whatever we could for you - and for any other staff that my brother might replace. I have not been unaware of your consideration for me."

The man nodded, his grey hair carefully swept back and lines forming at the sides of his eyes as he narrowed them a little.

"Forgive me for speaking frankly, my Lady. I am grateful to you." Turning back towards her, he gestured towards the wall opposite the door. "I do know, my Lady, that your brother has a hiding place behind that particular painting. It might be wise for you to look there." Julia stared at him, astounded at the butler's offer. "Forgive me if I am doing wrong."

"No, no!"

Exclaiming, she hurried forward, just as he made his way towards the painting in question. Julia found her hands pressed together against her lips as he pulled it back to reveal a small alcove behind it. She had not known it was there.

Her breath grew tight as she came closer, studying it carefully. There were only a few pieces of paper within it, as well as a few other things that she paid no heed to. Anything of value would be kept in other places in the house – places she knew well of since she had stolen and not yet returned such items from those places. Lifting one piece of paper from the other, she suddenly gasped aloud.

She had found it.

The study door opened once more and Julia let out a cry of fear, just as a footman came into the room.

"Forgive me for interrupting you, but the master has returned."

"Go at once, my Lady."

There was no time for her to wait nor to protest. Putting back the rest of the papers, but clinging to the only one of any importance, Julia fled from the room and left the butler to tidy the study. She could hear her brother's voice floating up from below stairs as she made her way to her bedchamber, running past one maid and a footman, who both stepped back out of her way. Shutting the door tightly, she twirled the key in the lock and then closed her eyes, her heart beating so fiercely that it hurt.

I have found it.

She had not been able to fully take it in when she had been in the study, but now she finally realized that everything she had worried about as regarded her brother was, in fact, the truth. This contract showed it. It was the one signed by Lord Wiltsham, the one which had given his money to her brother, who was pretending to be Baron March. And the writing upon it was very clearly her brother's hand – she would recognize it anywhere – as would many others. There was nothing her brother could say which would take away his guilt in this.

I have to get it to Lord Wiltsham.

"Julia?" Her brother hammered on the door and Julia let out a scream of fright, clutching the contract to her chest. "Julia, come out at once. There are guests."

Julia took a breath and closed her eyes.

"You startled me, brother! I will be out momentarily."

Her voice was shaking, but she kept as herself as contained as she could.

"I expect you in the drawing room within a few minutes, else I shall be back here to drag you down myself."

Saying nothing, Julia quickly folded up the contract, looking around the room for somewhere she might hide it. Making her way to her chest of drawers, she opened the drawer, only to see the pouch with the other items she had taken from her brother so long ago, still hidden within it. She had not yet returned them, and that sent another wedge of fear straight into her heart.

I cannot hide the contract here.

Looking around the room, she hurried towards her bed, lifting the sheets at the far end, and putting the folded contract underneath. It was all she could do for the present, knowing that her brother would most likely have the housekeeper open her bedroom door if she did not hurry downstairs as quickly as she could.

I must send a note to Lord Wiltsham as soon as I can. Hurrying from the room, she licked her lips as a bead of sweat ran down her spine, her heart beating furiously. *I know who has his fortune now. It is my own brother.*

CHAPTER FIFTEEN

"Lord Wiltsham. I have been looking everywhere for you."

Benjamin caught his breath as Miss Carshaw practically flung herself into his arms. Due to the crowd, he was able to wrap his arms around her waist for a moment and held her close, only to release her and capture both her hands in his.

"I confess I have been eager to see you also," he replied, but Miss Carshaw immediately shook her head. It was only then that Benjamin caught the paleness of her cheeks and the way that her eyes were wide with evident worry.

"It is true." Leaning closer, she kept her voice low. "It is all true. It is as you suspected. My brother is the one who has stolen your fortune." It was as if cold water had been flung into his face, and he struggled to take air into his tight lungs. His eyes fastened on hers, and she looked at him with steadiness, nodding gently when he blinked. "It is all as I have said," she promised him. "I know it to be true because I found a contract signed by your hand. The fortune was to be given to Baron March, was it not? That is the name that you told me, yes?"

Benjamin's chest was so tight that it was painful to take a breath. He had never imagined what this moment would be like, but it had come upon him now with such shock, it took all of his energy to give her a simple nod.

"The butler was able to help me," Miss Carshaw explained as her fingers squeezed his, perhaps hoping to initiate some response. "You cannot know of my surprise at his doing so. Indeed, I can barely find the words to explain my astonishment at his willingness, but I am entirely grateful for it. The contract was hidden in an alcove, behind a painting on the wall. The butler knew where such a thing was, whereas I did not. He has worked for my brother for a long time, but has always had a concern for me - for which I am grateful."

"As am I," Benjamin breathed, finally able to loosen his shoulders a little. "Where is this contract of his?"

It seems I will not have to attempt to mention the name of Baron March to Lord Kingston after all. I shall have the proof I require.

"It is safe back at my brother's townhouse. I thought to take it this evening, but I dared not do so for fear that my brother would somehow know that I was carrying something of significance. He has thrice asked me this evening whether or not I am well. It is as if he is suspicious that something is wrong."

Benjamin tilted his head.

"Mayhap you are a little pale and he noticed that only. Why else would he have such suspicions?" Benjamin murmured his thoughts aloud. "Unless he is concerned that I am a little too close to him, and will discover something about his behavior?"

Miss Carshaw licked her lips.

"And it may be that not all of his staff are as loyal to me as I might hope. I cannot pretend that they would all show me the same kindness as the butler. I was even warned of it."

Benjamin caught the flicker of worry dancing in her eyes.

"You were meant to write to me the moment that your brother left the house. I would have come to it in a moment, and you would have been spared this anxiety."

Miss Carshaw shook her head.

"There would have been very little point in my doing so. When it came to it, I realized that I was the best one to do such a thing, and thus I did. I must continue to hope that my brother does not know that I have found the contract and have it in my possession. At present it is tucked between the sheets in my bedchamber. I did not know where else to put it."

Benjamin shook his head to himself, hardly able to take in this momentous news, despite his concern for Miss Carshaw. Finally, he had the culprit revealed, all thanks to Miss Carshaw's determination and courage. What he was to do now, however, he did not know.

"I must give you this contract at once."

Pulled from his thoughts, Benjamin nodded, only to see Miss Carshaw's eyes widen and feel her fingers pulling at his. Realization slowly dawned.

"You want me to go with you now?"

"Yes, I cannot see a better time than this."

"We are in the middle of a soiree."

"And we shall not be missed," she insisted, beginning to move away, and given that his hand was still wrapped in hers, Benjamin found himself following her. Glancing around, Benjamin quickly caught the eye of Lord Foster who, in turn, lifted one eyebrow. Benjamin gave him a short nod, which Lord Foster returned, with a small gleam coming into his eyes, clearly aware that Benjamin was standing on the cusp of something great. Should any untoward words begin to swirl as to where he and Miss Carshaw had gone, Benjamin had no doubt that Lord Foster would find a way to make certain that Miss Carshaw's name remained unsullied. She had endured enough already. "Is your carriage here?"

Her eyes were desperately searching his as they stepped outside.

"Yes, of course it is." Snapping his fingers, he murmured something to a footman, who nodded and then hurried away. "It will be here within a few minutes, but we must consider whether or not this is for the best."

Miss Carshaw flung up her hands.

"There is no time for such thoughts! What is best for us both is that we confirm whether or not my brother has truly done such a thing. I wish to know for myself, as well as to discover whether or not you can regain your fortune. It is only fair that, if it has been taken from you by force, you once more find yourself in possession of it."

"I myself can make my way to your brother's house."

Shaking her head, she turned to face him.

"They would not let you into the house. Besides which, if my brother has done this, then I should do all within my power to right the wrong. I do not know what you can do once you have his copy of the contract in your hands, but at least you will have the proof. That must be something, at least."

The moon hid itself behind a cloud and Miss Carshaw shivered. Benjamin wrapped one arm around her shoulders, pulling her lightly against him. She was shivering, but he did not know whether it was from the cold, or from trepidation. Either way, his only thought was to comfort her.

"It is not your responsibility to right any wrongs, my dear Julia. I should never think ill of you for something that your brother has chosen to do."

"But I would think ill of myself." Turning her head, she looked up at him with only the flickering flames of a nearby torch illuminating her features. Her eyes were soft, drawing him towards her all the more. "I could not stand beside you as your wife, knowing that there was something more I could have done to remove us both from a situation of poverty; a situation that it now seems my brother has been an integral part of creating." Her head rested on his shoulder. "And I could not have both love and guilt in my heart, Lord Wiltsham. It would slowly drain me of life, I am sure."

In that very moment, it was as though the clouds had heard her speak, and fled from the moon as its gentle light illuminated them both. The fact that she had spoken of love made his heart tear asunder and slowly piece itself back together again with such joy that he could not speak for some moments, as he looked down into Miss Carshaw's face, and wished that he could find a way to describe every single piece of emotion which ran through him.

"This, then, is what it feels like to be in love."

Saying those words aloud, he caught Miss Carshaw's slight hitch of breath. Her eyes were wide, one hand settling to his chest as she twisted around so that she could look up into his face.

"You speak as I feel, Lord Wiltsham. I have seen the love between Lord Foster and Miss Lawrence, and often I have wondered what it feels like to be filled with such an emotion. Now, it seems I need wonder no longer."

The moon seemed to send flashes of light through the air around them as Miss Carshaw smiled, sending Benjamin's heart practically tearing out of his chest with joy.

"I find myself in the same position as you, my dear lady. I have spoken as I feel. Everything I say is the truth: I care for you so deeply that it *must* be nothing but love. My days are spent wondering when I will next be in your company, my eyes search for you desperately whenever I walk into a ballroom or a drawing room, or even when I am out taking a walk. My hands ache to hold you close, my heart sings whenever you are near. Yes, Miss Carshaw – Julia – it seems as though I am in love with you."

Her hands lifted to settle around his neck.

"And my heart echoes the very same."

The sound of wheels and horses' hooves prevented them from saying anything more and, much to Benjamin's frustration, Miss Carshaw was forced to step away. Nothing more could be said for the present, for as the carriage drew up, Benjamin urged Julia forward. Once they were seated, it drew away quickly, but Benjamin kept Julia near. His arm went again around her shoulders as her head nestled close on his chest.

"If I have you, I do not require a great fortune." Murmuring softly, he dropped a light kiss to her temple. "You are far more to me than any amount of coin. Regardless of what happens next, we shall be happy together, I have no doubt about it. Money cannot pay for the happiness we have found together. Even in poverty, I am certain that we will have joy."

Miss Carshaw lifted her head and looked straight into

his eyes. "We have something that no amount of money could ever purchase," she agreed. "And I will be more than content with that."

CHAPTER SIXTEEN

*S*crabbling under the blankets, Julia froze, her hands curling into the sheet.

It is not here. Where can it have gone?

Pulling back the sheets once more, she searched in vain for the contract where she had placed it, but to no avail. Her heart quickened its pace, as a sour taste grew in her mouth as she stepped back, a sudden furious fear billowing.

My brother. He must have found it.

One of the staff must have seen her entering or perhaps leaving the study, someone loyal to her brother, although she had no thought that the butler would have done such a thing. A maid perhaps, or even a footman? After all, she had run past two of them in the hallway on her way back from her brother's study.

"I do not know what to do."

Putting her hand to her forehead, she turned around, making her way to the chest of drawers where she had hidden those other valuable items. Had she changed her mind and placed the contract in there, only to forget about it? Opening the drawer, she looked through everything in it, but there was nothing there save for clothes, and the cloth bag with the valuables inside. Pulling it out, she spread the items on her the bed, wanting to make quite certain that she had not made any mistake. The pearls, the diamond earrings, the signet ring, the gold bracelets, and her father's watch – an item which held no monetary value but was of great sentiment to her. *And yet, no contract. I did not put it here.* Placing the items carefully back in the cloth bag, she shook her head, her eyes burning. The contract had vanished. The only thing she had to prove that her brother had stolen Lord Wiltsham's fortune was gone. What was she to do now?

A sudden sound echoed through the open door and Julia caught her breath, whirling around without so much as putting the cloth bag back in her drawer. She hurried from the room, having no need to ask what the commotion was all about.

Her brother had returned to the house.

His voice seemed to fill every single space within the building and Julia shuddered violently as she made her way down the staircase, wanting desperately to wrap herself in Lord Wiltsham's tight embrace so that he might shield her from the mockery and disdain she was certain her brother would throw her way.

"Is there any explanation as to why you and Lord Wiltsham are currently alone in my house?"

Her brother jabbed one finger in Lord Wiltsham's direction as Julia hurried into the room. Lord Wiltsham was sitting quite calmly in one of the drawing room chairs, a measure of brandy in a glass on a table by his side. He smiled at her, and Julia went forward, going to stand behind him and setting one hand on his shoulder. The peaceful look on his face was enough to calm her frantic thoughts for, if Lord Wiltsham was quite calm, then what had she to fear?

"I believe that your sister was coming in search of something important. Of course, I was more than happy to accompany her, since I was certain that *you* would have no interest in returning here."

Reaching up, Lord Wiltsham touched her fingers with his and Julia took great comfort from the simple gesture. Drawing in another breath, she closed her eyes briefly, steeling herself, and trying to regain the courage and fortitude that she had so often required in the face of her brother's disdain.

"And what is it that you left behind, my *dear* sister?"

Her brother knew all too well what she had come in search of, she was sure, but clearly, he was unwilling to be entirely honest with her. This was all part of his scheme, she realized. A scheme to hide the truth, just as he had been doing for so long.

"I think you already know brother." Lifting her chin, she squeezed Lord Wiltsham's shoulder lightly. "Why you felt the need to hide what I had already found, I cannot imagine."

Her brother continued to maintain a rather confused, somewhat astonished expression.

"I do not know what you mean."

"Of course you do." Lord Wiltsham shrugged. "You may choose to continue to refute it, but your sister and I both know exactly what it is that she discovered."

Becoming a little angry, Julia watched as her brother spread his hands, maintaining that entirely innocent expression. The way his eyes glinted lit more flames within her soul and she lifted her chin, glaring at him.

"I found your contract, brother. Your contract that claims Lord Wiltsham's fortune for your own."

"Contract?" He shrugged. "I have many contracts. You must be a little more specific – as well as telling me why you decided to search through my private things!"

Ignoring the latter part of this, Julia threw up her hands.

"You know very well what I am talking about. There is no need to hide it from me. The contract you had Lord Wiltsham sign when his mind was, no doubt, muddled by whatever it was you had given him in his brandy."

Her brother shook his head, as if pitying her.

"But I had never met Lord Wiltsham before, not until I realized he was interested in courting you. I find your accusations and your words very strange indeed."

She shook her head.

"Your pretense does not convince me, and what you have said as regards your first meeting with Lord Wiltsham I do not believe to be true. As I have said, you need not deny it."

Lord Wiltsham cleared his throat.

"You have been very eager to push your sister away from me."

"That is because I had plans for her to wed Lord Bullfield."

Julia's lips tightened for a moment, aware that all her brother would do was deny all that she threw at him. Without the contract, she had no proof.

"Your words make very little sense. You told me that I had a month to find a suitor, only to then insist that I wed Lord Bullfield when Lord Wiltsham appeared interested in courting me. There must have been a reason for that."

Her brother cleared his throat.

"My reasons are my own." He shifted on his feet, that

confidence seeping out of his expression. "I did not consider Lord Wiltsham suitable."

"But you just stated that you had never met me until that day when you walked into the drawing room and saw me in conversation with your sister," Lord Wiltsham put in, immediately. "What was it that you found so unsuitable within those few minutes between meeting me and calling your sister to your study to inform her of your intention to wed her to Lord Bullfield?"

Lord Kingston's jaw tightened.

"These questions are irrelevant. You are to wed my sister, are you not?"

The slight wobble in his voice made Julia smile softly. He was no longer as confident nor as polished as he had been before. The more questions they threw at him, the more he seemed to struggle.

"I find the question pertinent. I believe you *had* met me before, and whatever it was that you put in my brandy that evening made certain that I did not remember you."

"I did not. There is no contract to speak of. I have signed nothing. I have never met you before, and certainly would never even *consider* taking your fortune from you."

There came a short silence.

"You are an entirely selfish creature, brother. You may protest, but I believe that you would do exactly what I have stated. I have seen you change these last few years. I have seen you become more grasping, even though you have been given great wealth."

Her brother pressed one hand to his heart.

"You injure me, Julia."

"No more than you have injured me. The *ton* speak of you as though you are a cruel sort, and one to be cautious around, and now I realize that everything they have said about you is quite true."

"No, it is not."

His voice was a little higher now.

"You have stolen Lord Wiltsham's fortune."

Speaking a little more forcefully, she pointed one finger at him.

"I certainly did nothing of the sort."

"You made your way to the East End of London."

"I did not."

"You put something in his drink that evening."

Her brother shook his head, but his eyes darted around the room.

"You speak nothing of sense."

"And when the time came, you had him sign a document."

"What document?"

She continued on, pressing forward.

"And you pretended to be Baron Marsh."

"Baron March," her brother snapped, correcting her without thinking about what he was saying, and Julia shot one eyebrow towards the ceiling.

Silence fell.

Her fired questions, one after the other, had caused him to make a mistake. He had corrected her when he ought to have denied even knowing that name, and there was no escape for him now. Letting out her breath slowly, Julia heard Lord Wiltsham also blow out a long sigh as his shoulders relaxed. The truth was out, and none could hide from it now.

Julia looked straight at her brother as he gazed back at her, his cheeks a little pale. It was clear that he did not want to look in Lord Wiltsham's direction.

"It seems, then, that you know exactly what I am talking about it." Keeping her voice low, Julia lifted both hands. "You cannot have known that name unless you had written it yourself."

"You cannot pretend any longer," Lord Wiltsham added, his voice low. "Where did you put the contract?"

Lord Kingston opened his mouth, perhaps to protest his innocence again, only to catch the sharp eye of Lord Wiltsham. He dropped his head and drew in a breath. When he lifted it again, his eyes were darker than Julia had ever seen them, the slash of red around his mouth making her shiver.

"Given that the contract is mine, there is no need for you to either have it or know of its whereabouts."

Now, it seemed, he was no longer able to deny that he had written the contract but was instead demanding that he keep it entirely to himself.

Lord Wiltsham cleared his throat.

"You have admitted that you are Baron March. I am aware of what you did that evening, and your relationship with Lord Montague and his wicked schemes. You may think of yourself as successful, but that coin is not yours. It was taken from me at a time when I could not consent to it. You have no right to keep the money."

"Particularly when you have more than enough wealth of your own," Julia put in, at which her brother began to laugh.

The darkness in his eyes shifted to his voice and Julia shivered, just as Lord Wiltsham reached up to grasp her hand with his.

"And do you truly believe, sister, that our father left us with enough wealth to be comfortable?" he asked, his dark eyes flashing. "As I have said, father was not a frugal man. I shall have to work hard to make sure that the estate is profitable, and that the wealth I have at present continues to increase."

Julia looked back at him steadily. The way he had admitted to taking such wealth had come as a great astonishment to her. It was as though he genuinely believed that he had every right to take what belonged to others.

"And you think that you can do so by drugging unwitting gentlemen and taking their fortunes whilst they are indisposed, simply to secure your own wealth? I do not believe that you are poor, brother. I believe that you have an evil desire to hold onto as much coin as you can, and that you will get it in any way that you can."

"A gentleman must do what he must to protect his own estate."

Lord Kingston drew himself up, folding his arms across his chest and lifting his chin, as if daring either of them to challenge him.

"It seems to me that rather than doing whatever you could to make your estate profitable by way of your own hard work, you decided instead to steal what did not belong to you," Lord Wiltsham interrupted, pushing himself up to stand, before Julia could say anything more. "Is that not so? Perhaps I am not even the first to have felt the sting of your deception."

Julia practically felt the heat from her brother's glare, despite the distance between them, but Lord Wiltsham managed to simply ignore it.

"Regardless as to whether or not you have a vast deal of coin or very little, it is a gentleman's duty to work hard at his estate and to make it as profitable as it can be – through legitimate means. If a gentleman's main concern is that his wealth might not be enough to keep it prosperous, then such a gentleman of honor would work at his *own* estate on his *own* land to make sure that it was safe and secure for generations to come. You, on the other hand, have simply decided to take what is not yours, so that you might become successful – or all the richer. There is no honor in that."

Lord Wiltsham's hand touched hers and she quickly laced her fingers through his so that they stood as one.

"To be truthful, I cannot believe that you are as impoverished as you make out. I do not think that there was a single, legitimate reason for you to take even a penny from another. Rather, I believe that you did so simply because you are selfish, because you are greedy, and because you are too lazy to make any effort to work hard. It is easier for you to steal than to put everything you have into your estate."

Julia caught her breath. She could not imagine what her brother was going to say to her words, but from the darkness in his eyes, she trusted it would not be of any jot of contrition. He had despised every word.

"I knew that I was wise to take your wealth."

Lord Kingston was obviously furious, the arrogance and condescension sweeping toward Julia as she stared at her brother, horrified by his response and the clear contempt within his voice. There was no hiding the truth now, and yet, even though she had known of it, upon hearing him say it aloud, her heart still shattered.

"It is clear that you have not even the smallest amount of sympathy for others, nor regret for what you have done," Lord Wiltsham replied, his voice still low, but steady regardless. "I will, however, expect you to return my fortune to me. You know as well as I that it was taken from me without my consent, and certainly without my awareness."

He spoke so quietly, and with such a great calm that Julia's heart no longer beat as rapidly as it had done before.

Instead, she almost felt calm too, quite sure that her brother would not be able to refuse.

That calm fled as the laughter which rattled from her brother's lips froze her very bones, as she heard the twist of mockery through it. Lord Wiltsham, however, did not react, save but to tighten his fingers on hers.

"You really are a fool if you think that I will give you anything which I now consider to be my own. There is no need for me to do so, so therefore I shall not."

Lord Wiltsham tilted his head.

"Then you have no concern about the fact that you will be sending your sister into a life of poverty."

It did not come as a surprise when her brother immediately shrugged, although Julia's heart still twisted at the lack of consideration he showed her. She should have expected it, after the last few years, yet somehow, it still hurt.

"She has made her choice. Why should anything my sister does now concern me?"

"Perhaps because she is your sister, as well as the fact that you made a promise to your father to take care of those he has left behind." Another gentle squeeze came. "Mis Carshaw has told me of it."

"I have no doubt that she embellished a great deal," Kingston sneered, flinging out one hand towards her dispassionately. "As far as I am concerned, I have taken excellent care of my sister. It is hardly my fault if she wishes to behave in such a ridiculously foolish manner by marrying a gentleman who can offer her no security."

"Security that *you* have taken from us, rather than he," Julia protested, but Lord Wiltsham merely pressed her fingers again, silencing any further remarks.

If her brother was not to agree to return his fortune,

then did Lord Wiltsham have another plan as to how to regain it? How would they manage?

"I had someone for you, Julia. I sent Lord Bullfield to you, knowing that he was a gentleman who was able to care for you as you deserved, but you rejected him! That is on your own head."

Despite the press to her fingers, Julia shook her head.

"That is hardly fair. You expect me to be grateful that for a gentleman such as Lord Bullfield, as though he is known to be a paragon of gentlemanly integrity! You know as well as I that he is nothing but cruelty itself. No. I know you possess not even a modicum of consideration for me – you stood to gain something in the match, that is all."

"You have no proof of any such thing," her brother spat, his face flushed and hot. "This conversation is at an end. There is nothing we need speak about any longer." His eyes turned to Lord Wiltsham. "You will not be able to regain your fortune, Lord Wiltsham, no matter the strength of your determination. I have made certain that the contract, which you believed my sister had, was discovered. It has been returned to me, and you will never see it again. Make your way back to the ball, Julia. There is nothing else for you here."

Looking into her brother's eyes, Julia found herself weak with hopelessness. It was not the fact that she wanted her brother to be able to restore Lord Wiltsham's fortune simply for the fortune's sake, but rather because the man she loved had nothing other than what her wicked brother had determined he should have - which was very little indeed. She felt that to be so deeply wrong that her heart ached, and she looked desperately towards Lord Wiltsham, wanting him to offer her something which could be done, but he merely shrugged his shoulders and smiled.

"There is nothing to be done, but I am glad that I have discovered where my fortune has gone," he murmured, quietly. "You know very well that my thoughts are not centered on regaining it. If I have you by my side, then we will find a way through whatever faces us in our future, one way or the other."

Julia shook her head, eager to find a way to force her brother's hand. It did not seem right that evil should win.

"Listen to Lord Wiltsham, Julia. You have not got the contract, so therefore you cannot prove anything to anyone. It is better for you to return with him to the ball and enjoy whatever you can of the evening. I doubt you will be able to attend many social occasions in the years to come."

Julia dropped her head forward. Alas, it seemed that her brother was correct, for if she did not have the contract, then she could not prove anything to anyone, even if they wished to.

"This does not seem right, but what else is there for us to do?"

Lord Wiltsham smiled down at her as her brother chuckled darkly at the other end of the room.

"If we make certain that our life is not one of misery, if we have each other, then that will be a happiness which none can take from us. I shall still have to find a new seal, of course, given that my signet ring is most likely in the hands of your brother, but that can be easily done. Whatever we must face, we will face together."

Julia caught her breath, her hands going to her mouth. Why had she never realized before? Without another word, she dashed from the room, hurrying away, and ignoring the cries of her brother and Lord Wiltsham, who were undoubtedly wondering where she was going. Her heart hammering furiously, she made her way up to her bedchamber, pulled open the drawer, then recalled that she had left the cloth bag on the bed. Turning, she found what she was searching for in a matter of seconds, and running back towards the drawing room, threw the door open, then rushed towards Lord Wiltsham.

"Your signet ring. This is it, is it not?" Waiting until he had opened his hand, she set it down in his palm, seeing the widening of his eyes as he took it. "That has been in my brother's possession for many weeks. I will testify to it to anyone who will listen. The town will know of what my brother has done. Yes, there will be a scandal, and I am quite certain that I shall be tainted by it, but I care not. My brother should not be allowed to behave in this manner, and believe that he can find success." Spinning around, she faced her brother, her hands going to her hips. "You have not been successful. I have discovered my betrothed's signature on a document within your own house – and I have no doubt that I will find the contract once I have had time to search for it again, regardless of where your loyal footman has put it. Your guilt will be known to society, brother, I will make sure of it. I will tell this sordid tale to every gossip amongst the dragons of the *ton*, and they will lap it up, and tell everyone else. What will you do when they all turn their back on you? It is not as though you have a sterling reputation already. Many a gentleman knows to avoid your company. How low you will sink in their estimation now!"

Her brother's eyes narrowed, and for a moment Julia thought that he was going to laugh. But his lips did not curve, and much to her surprise, he made a start forward, as if he intended to grasp the signet ring from Lord Wiltsham's hand - but then he stepped back. Lord Wiltsham dropped the signet ring into an inner pocket of his coat as Lord Kingston turned to glare at Julia.

"You are foolish indeed, Julia. You think that the *ton* will believe you? That they will take your word to be the truth?"

"I should think it would be very surprising for a young lady to declare her brother to be a thief," Lord Wiltsham replied. "Indeed, it would be so very odd that I am certain that most of the *ton* would believe her words."

Again, his voice remained mild, but the triumph building in Julia's heart could not be removed. Her brother knew that he was facing difficulty now, for she could tell from his growing frown and the narrowing of his eyes.

"The only way to salvage your reputation is to return Lord Wiltsham's fortune. Show that you have even an ounce of credibility within you." Lifting her chin, she squeezed Lord Wiltsham's hand gently. "It is over, brother. You have failed."

"Perhaps." Clearing his throat, Lord Kingston spread his hands. "What say you, Lord Wiltsham. I *will* return your fortune to you - every single penny - but on one condition."

"You are hardly in the position to bargain with me," came the reply, but Lord Kingston held up for one hand, silencing Lord Wiltsham.

"What say you?" he asked again, ignoring the question. "I shall return your fortune on one condition."

"And what would that condition be?"

Julia scowled as her brother smiled, noting the cruel glint in his eyes and the confidence in his smile, as though he believed that he would have every success.

"You shall have every penny returned to you the moment you break the betrothal to my sister."

CHAPTER SEVENTEEN

The thud of Benjamin's heart was so loud that the room seemed to echo with sound. Lord Kingston stared at him, perhaps believing that what he had offered was going to be fully accepted by Benjamin at any moment, but Benjamin shook his head, letting out a disbelieving laugh.

Lord Kingston's smile faded.

"This may come as an astonishment to you, but there is nothing you could say to me that would induce me to give up your sister. It is not even a consideration."

"Then you are a fool," Lord Kingston retorted. "I have offered you a chance to regain your fortune and you push it aside in favor of my sister. Your entire future hinges on this decision! Will you truly give up security and safety for *her?*" Flinging out one hand, he dismissed Julia in a moment. "You shall come to regret this."

Benjamin shook his head.

"I shall *never* regret choosing your sister over any amount of money. We have what you shall never possess, and it is something that you shall never be able to take away."

Lord Kingston merely laughed.

"And what help can that be when you are cold and shivering, struggling to find enough coal to heat the fire? Will you be glad of your choice then?"

"I shall continue to be glad," Benjamin stated firmly, releasing Miss Carshaw's hand, but instead pulling her close to him with one hand around her waist. "That is the problem, Kingston. You cannot understand. You have no capacity for understanding because of what it is that we possess. I do not think that you will ever be able to fully grasp it and for that, I am rather sorry."

Lord Kingston's jaw was working hard, and the laugh he attempted to force out was only a rough broken cackle, although Benjamin did his best not to outwardly react as Lord Kingston tried to laugh again, seeing that from him as nothing more than sheer cruelty indeed. To be so dismissive of his sister must be causing her great pain, and he wanted very much to wrap his arms around Julia and protect her from such an obvious and calculated wickedness.

"I have given you the opportunity and you have not taken it." Lord Kingston threw his arms asunder. "There is nothing else that can be done. Might I suggest that you leave this house, Lord Wiltsham, and take my sister with you for the moment."

Beside him, Benjamin heard Miss Carshaw splutter as he fought to find something to say in response. Lord Kingston had confessed to so much, but there appeared to be no consequences for him.

"You know that Lord Wiltsham and I will speak of the signet ring and what you have done. The gossip will spread."

Lord Kingston shrugged.

"You state that you shall do so, certainly, but I will do all I can to defend myself. Mayhap I shall state that you were simply unwilling to wed, and that this is your response to my insistence. Have no doubt, I shall find a way, sister, to preserve my reputation."

There did not seem to be anything else that could be said. Benjamin looked at Miss Carshaw, seeing the frustration in her eyes, and wishing desperately that he could find a way to bring them both a sense of justice. Certainly, he found this a difficult and trying situation, but Lord Kingston was not his brother. He could not imagine the stress and strain that burdened her now.

"Come, my dear. Let us make our way back to the ball."

Holding one hand out to Miss Carshaw, he waited for a few moments until she finally nodded. Her eyes were fixed on her brother, her jaw had tightened, and her face was devoid of color. When she grasped his hand, it was as with a grip as tight as any he had ever felt.

Walking from the room with their heads held high and no words spoken was no easy task, but Benjamin achieved it, nonetheless. Miss Carshaw's hand was still tight to his, clear anger still burning in her face as they made their way into the hallway

"I feel as much as you do, but there is nothing to be done. We must simply enjoy the ball this evening and think about what we are to do thereafter. As I have said, I am sure that we can find a way forward, even in the difficulties of poverty."

She stopped suddenly, pulling his arm backwards.

"Wait a moment." She looked up him, her eyes wide. "Think on what we are to do thereafter..."

Little understanding of what it was that he had either

said or done to bring about such a reaction, Benjamin looked at her for a long moment, waiting for her to explain, but she did not. Instead, whirling around, she left him standing in the hallway, making her way above stairs, and almost dragging the astonished butler after her. Benjamin did not call for her to return, trusting that she would do so when she was ready. Pulling his signet ring from his pocket, he slipped it once more onto the smallest finger of his right hand and turned his hand this way and that so that he might look at it - not so that he might admire it, however. This has been passed on through generations for decades and the relief that now filled him at having it back on his finger again was substantial. He pushed his head back, his shoulders shifting so that he might breathe a little more easily.

At least I know now who has stolen my fortune, even if I am unable to have it returned to me.

That brought him a little comfort, Benjamin had to admit, albeit with the awareness that he would not be able to provide any sort of satisfaction for Miss Carshaw. She would face a life of difficulty as wife to a gentleman who had no fortune, thanks to the selfishness of her brother. All the same, he was glad that the truth had been revealed to him. He would not have to spend his days wondering what was to be done, any longer.

Miss Carshaw appeared soon afterward with a small bag in her hand. She did not say a word, but took his hand and hurried outside, drawing him after her, making her way immediately towards the carriage as though she had not a moment to lose. Benjamin went quickly with her, rather glad to be leaving her brother's house. Those who had warned him about the man had been quite correct to do so. There was something about Lord Kingston which was deeply unpleasant.

The carriage pulled away, and Benjamin leaned his head back, finding Miss Carshaw's hand in the darkness and grasping it tightly.

"I am sorry, Julia."

Her fingers laced through his.

"You need not apologize. None of what occurred was your fault. It has been my brother's behavior entirely. You are not to place any blame upon your shoulders."

There was a lightness to her voice that he had not expected to hear.

"Julia, I –"

"Besides which," she continued as though she had not heard him. "I believe that my brother may soon change his mind. In fact, I expect him to call upon you very soon."

He did not ask what was to occur, seeing a slight glint in her eye and praying silently that she knew what she was doing. After all, she was the one who would know her brother best.

"Whatever you have set in motion, I beg of you to be careful." There was a darkness to Lord Kingston, but perhaps none of them had expected to see the full depths of it. Considering it, Benjamin's concern mounted for her all the more. "Do not test your brother. Your safety must be the only consideration in all of this."

To his surprise, Miss Carshaw chuckled, her hand grasping his.

"I know my brother, Lord Wiltsham. There is something that he will not be able to ignore; something that he will do anything to regain. Trust me. I have found a way to regain your fortune. I am more than sure of it."

It was the following afternoon that a knock came at Benjamin's door. Lord Foster, Lord Stoneleigh, and himself were present, as well as Miss Lawrence and Miss Carshaw, who had come to join them for the afternoon. There had been much talk of everything which had taken place, but for whatever reason, Miss Carshaw appeared almost buoyant, quite certain that all would be well. She had not explained anything to Benjamin, but he was slowly beginning to trust that whatever plan she had in place would be a success. His heart claimed a good deal more confidence in her than he had expected, and her bright smile and dancing eyes brought him great relief. She was not overly perturbed by all that her brother had done, it seemed, and whatever it was she intended, it appeared that she had every expectation that it would go in their favor.

"My Lord, you have a visitor," his butler intoned as he came into the room. "Viscount Kingston."

He handed him the card and Benjamin flipped it over, pretending to be interested in the arrival of the fellow whilst his heart immediately quickened its pace.

"Did he say what he wanted?" he asked as the butler shook his head. "Then pray send him in."

Immediately, Benjamin's gaze went to Miss Carshaw but, rather than fear, there was a gentle smile on her lips. She appeared filled with a confidence that seemed to spread through the room and into Benjamin's own heart.

"Where is it?" Lord Kingston practically threw himself into the room, his gaze narrowed as he turned to glare at Benjamin. "Did my sister inform you of its value? How dare you take something that belongs to me?"

The irony of that particular statement made Benjamin roll his eyes, whilst Lord Foster rose from his chair.

"I do not think we have been introduced," he said easily.

"You must be the lying, scheming, dishonorable, despicable gentleman who has stolen Lord Wiltsham's fortune."

"I do not have time for pleasantries," the man spat, barely flicking a gaze towards him. "Where is it, Wiltsham? Return it to me this instant."

"I do not know what you speak of," Benjamin replied honestly. "What is it that I must return to you?"

Was this why Miss Carshaw had said nothing? She wanted him to be able to speak honestly in front of her brother.

"The practically *priceless* diamond necklace, which is my family's heirloom," Lord Kingston replied, jabbing one finger in Benjamin's direction. "You were in my house last evening so you must have taken it."

He did not notice Miss Carshaw's quiet voice through his exclamations, and it was only when she stepped forward that he finally realized she was present in the room.

"Do not lay any blame upon Lord Wiltsham, brother." Her voice was calm as she walked toward him. "Did you truly think that I would simply allow you to continue with this scheme as though you were quite able to do such a thing without consequences? Did you not hear Lord Wiltsham last evening? We have a great and immovable affection for each other, one which surpasses all else. Were you so foolish as to believe that even if I *could* do something about the situation, I would not do so? You are quite mistaken in that, Kingston. I will do whatever is required to return what you stole from him to my betrothed."

"You will return that to me at once."

Lord Kingston's lips had gone white with anger as he took a step forward, but Miss Carshaw merely shook her head.

"No, I shall not. Why should I do so, given that you have refused to return what you have stolen?"

Lord Kingston threw up his hands in evident exasperation.

"That is not yours to take! You cannot simply lay claim to what is mine, not without consequence."

"Which is precisely what I believe can be said to you also." Benjamin smiled at her determination and came to stand beside her, looking to Lord Kingston with naught but pride in his heart for the lady next to him. She was nothing but wonderful, refusing to be cowed in the face of her brother's darkness. "Did you truly believe that I would marry Lord Wiltsham without doing anything and everything I could to regain what my brother stole from him?" she continued, speaking clearly and very distinctly. "I do not do so for my own comfort, but because it is the *right* thing for me to do. I could not have lived beside Lord Wiltsham, knowing that his struggle was because of you, because of what you had taken from the man that I love. My conscience will not permit me to do so. Therefore, I have taken something of great value that belongs solely to you, so that you will return what is of value to Lord Wiltsham. I will not say it is of the greatest value, for we have found something much more precious than money could ever buy, whereas money is all that you have."

Benjamin watched and listened, as the courage he had seen so often in her before reached an even higher strength. Her emerald gaze was dazzling; the proud tilt of her head one that brought admiration. Lord Kingston's cruelty could not stand in the face of her quick wits, her fortitude, and her love for Benjamin.

"You know all too well the value of that necklace," Lord Kingston spat, his eyes like dark hollows. "That has long been in our family. You are stealing from your own kin, from those who have entrusted you to care for such items. How can you turn your back on them now?"

His harsh words did not send even a spark of guilt into her eyes.

"It is not I who ought to question my behavior, brother." Placing her hands on her hips, she tilted her head. "To take an almost priceless heirloom is one thing, but to just behave in a manner which brings shame on the family name is something else entirely. My conscience was not pricked even a little. My heart has cried out over the change in your character these last years. I believe that when the family fortune became yours, Kingston, you have found yourself not master of it, but almost slave to it instead, driven to forcefully seek to gain as much as you possibly can for yourself. That eagerness has torn any kindness from you, and now I fear that there is nothing which can be done to save your slowly darkening heart."

One look towards Lord Kingston and Benjamin could tell that his sister's words had dealt him a great blow, although Lord Kingston attempted to cover it up just as quickly as he could. There was a pallor to Lord Kingston's cheeks now and his eyes were no longer narrowed. Instead, he stared at Miss Carshaw as though he had never expected her to speak with such vehemence - which, to Benjamin's mind, simply declared all the more that the man did not know his sister very well at all; that he believed his authority was all that was required to make certain his sister obeyed. Had he learned nothing these last few months? Had he not seen Miss Carshaw's courage in the same way that Benjamin had? To him, it was one of her most admirable traits, but to Lord Kingston, it would be quite the opposite.

It took Lord Kingston some moments to regain himself.

On three occasions, he attempted to speak, only to swallow and look away. After much coughing and clearing of the throat, he shook his head and once more, pointed one finger at Miss Carshaw.

"If you do not return it, you shall not wed Lord Wiltsham."

There was a quiet feebleness to his voice, and before Benjamin could give any retort, Miss Carshaw let out a sorrowful laugh.

"How weak you are, brother. Do you still think that you can make such threats and have them mean anything to me?" Leaning against Benjamin but keeping her eyes trained on her brother, she shook her head. "You may forbid me all you wish, but if you do so, then I shall simply elope. You may lock me in my room for all I care, but I will still find a way. You cannot separate us. Your threats mean nothing. They are as dust."

Lord Foster and Lord Stoneleigh rose to their feet, coming a little closer to Lord Kingston.

"Your threats are not welcome here," Lord Foster stated, his gaze steadily fixed on Lord Kingston. "Your reputation is already sullied. Do you truly wish to add our voices to those who disdain you, and tell others of that disdain? When it comes to your own time to wed – for you will be required to do so to produce the heir - I sincerely doubt that you will find any young lady willing to take your hand, given the rumors that are already spread about you."

Benjamin saw the slight droop in Lord Kingston's posture.

"You have no choice, Kingston. Either you return my fortune to me, and your sister will return the necklace, or you do not, and we continue as we are, each in possession of something we ought not to have. Decide what you will do and, regardless of what your choice is, I can promise you that Julia and I will be more than content."

Lord Kingston said nothing, keeping his eyes fixed on his sister for some moments, as though he expected her to change her mind. But when she did not, he glowered at them each in turn, his lips white with fury, before turning and making his way from the room directly, slamming the door behind him. The sound echoed around the room and Miss Carshaw let out a deep and heavy sigh, turning so that her head nestled into his neck, Benjamin slipped one arm around her waist and drew her close, only then realizing the full extent of what she had done, and the strength of mind required to do it.

"My admiration for you knows no bounds," he murmured against her temple. "You are a woman of great courage. You have such fortitude and uprightness of heart which will not allow you to see or be satisfied with injustice. The depth of love you have for me within your heart is so obvious that it has me spellbound. That you would go to such lengths for me means more to me than I can express."

Miss Carshaw heaved another sigh, leaning against him even more as he held her close.

"I could not simply allow him to continue with such evil and to be victorious in his wickedness. I do not know whether I shall succeed, but at least now there is a little hope."

Benjamin chuckled.

"You are aware that we cannot keep the necklace, even if he does *not* decide to return my fortune?"

Miss Carshaw lifted her head and looked into his eyes, a smile on her lips.

"My intention was never to keep it, only to use it to regain what is rightly yours. I did not tell you for fear that your honorable heart would not permit me to do such a thing in the first place, but now that it has occurred, let us hope that it is enough to bring success."

"And if it does not, then you are not to carry any guilt," he told her, as Lord Foster and Lord Stoneleigh turned away so that Benjamin and Miss Carshaw might have as much privacy as could be afforded. "You have done all that you can and more. We shall not carry this burden any longer. There is only to be joy from now on."

Smiling, Miss Carshaw dropped her head back to his shoulder, her other arm going around him and, at that moment, Benjamin felt his joy complete.

EPILOGUE

"I have heard everything that took place." Miss Lawrence glanced at Julia as they walked together through the park. "You cannot imagine my surprise to hear of all that you have done. I am in awe of your courage."

Julia shook her head.

"It was of no great consequence. I believe that anyone would have done the same, had they the opportunity or requirement! You will understand it when I say to you that to see the person one loves most in the world so injured is not a bearable situation."

Miss Lawrence nodded solemnly.

"I quite agree."

"Lord Wiltsham has told me I must not do anything more." Looking down at the path for a moment, Julia's lips twisted. "He states that I have done all I can, and he is quite right to state so. But nonetheless, I am praying daily that my brother will do what is right. We have no intention of keeping the necklace, regardless of what he chooses to do. It will be returned whether he gives Lord Wiltsham back his fortune or not although, of course, my brother does not know that." A long breath escaped her. "I will not be as my brother is."

Her heart twisted again, all the more painfully.

Julia was all too aware of the great risk she had taken in stealing the diamond necklace. It was of extraordinary value, and an heirloom that had been passed from generation to generation. It had been the one thing that Julia had chosen to leave behind when she had first thought about escaping her brother's house. To her mind, it was of too great a consequence to take for herself.

However, in this situation, taking it was an action meant to force her brother's hand. When the thought had come to her, she had not hesitated, but had acted on instinct, rushing to her brother's study in search of it. Even as she had picked it up, Julia had known that she would return it. She had understood that at the moment when she had laid hands on it. Her brother was a thief, but she was not about to make herself a thief as well. It would be used as a bargaining chip, nothing more. And if her brother did not respond as she hoped, then it would be given back to him, and she and Lord Wiltsham would find another way through their difficulties. It certainly had forced her brother to think, however, but whether it would be enough to force him to do as they had asked, they were yet to find out.

"How long has it been?"

"A sennight."

Each day had drifted past with agonizing slowness.

"And you have remained in the house with him?"

"I have." Julia shrugged. "I have nothing to fear from him. He knows that now - he is fully aware that there is nothing he can say which will tear me from Lord Wiltsham's side. There is nothing that he can do which would force me to obey him."

"I am sure, also, that he did not take well to you saying that to him."

A wry smile crossed her lips.

"Indeed, he did not. But for once there is nothing for him to say. All we need now is to wait to see whether or not he will respond."

"Even that must be something of a trial." Miss Lawrence smiled softly. "You are doing very well."

"I have Lord Wiltsham to thank for my composure. He is everything that I need and more."

The sudden sound of running footsteps - which was a most extraordinary thing to hear in the midst of Hyde Park – had both she and Miss Lawrence turning around swiftly to see where the sound was coming from.

Her name was then shouted in the most extraordinary fashion and before she could react in any way, strong arms flung around her waist, and she was being swung around.

Wiltsham.

Her hands went around Lord Wiltsham's neck as she clung to him, laughing as he looked down into her face and then put her down gently.

"You are causing quite an uproar, Lord Wiltsham," she laughed as he steadied her. "Whatever is the meaning of all of this?"

"I have it!" Heedless of those around him, Lord Wiltsham cupped her face with both hands, his eyes sparkling with obvious joy. "I have it, Julia. I received word from my solicitors today."

It took her a moment to realize what he meant, but when it finally came to her, she could not quite take it in.

Her eyes rounded as her hands clung to his jacket as he nodded, still beaming at her.

"You mean to say that –"

"Yes, I have regained my fortune. Your brother has chosen to return it all to me – which means that we must give him the necklace, of course - but we have succeeded. *You* have succeeded. Your plan has worked, Julia. You have defeated your brother and we no longer need to worry about our future."

Julia's breath was ragged as she stared into his face. It was as if her heart did not want to believe it, as if she dared not let herself trust it was true. But the hope in his eyes and the tightness of his hands around her waist told her that she had nothing left to fear.

"My brother has conceded?"

Her whispered words made Lord Wiltsham laugh.

"Yes, my darling, your brother has conceded. He could not battle against your wit and determination. You have succeeded where I could not, you have found a way forward for us both. We shall have stability, and I will be able to care for you as a husband ought."

"You would have been able to do so without your money," Julia replied as he smiled at her. "It is our love for each other that will give us all that we require."

"Yes, that is quite so." Lord Wiltsham dipped his head and caught her lips in a breathless kiss that had him stealing her breath. No doubt there would be uproar amongst society, for there were plenty of witnesses, but Julia did not care. The only thing she wanted was to be in Lord Wiltsham's arms and to have him hold her close, complete in the joy of knowing they would never have such difficulties again. "I love you, Julia." Lord Wiltsham whispered against her mouth, one hand brushing across her cheek, the other wrapped around her waist. "From the moment I first found you in my house, I believe that my heart has belonged to you. I cannot and will not be separated from you ever again. I love you with all of my heart."

Julia smiled up at him, her heart full to overflowing. The fact that they would never be separated again was a balm to her heart, her pain and troubles soothed away to peace and happiness.

"I want always to be in your arms, Wiltsham," she murmured softly. "I love you too."

Julia and Lord Wilsham met in an unusual way but I am so glad it all worked out for them! Check out the first book in the series A Viscount's Stolen Fortune. Read ahead for a sneak peek!

MY DEAR READER

Thank you for reading and supporting my books! I hope this story brought you some escape from the real world into the always captivating Regency world. A good story, especially one with a happy ending, just brightens your day and makes you feel good! If you enjoyed the book, would you leave a review on Amazon? Reviews are always appreciated.

Below is a complete list of all my books! Why not click and see if one of them can keep you entertained for a few hours?

The Duke's Daughters Series
The Duke's Daughters: A Sweet Regency Romance Boxset
A Rogue for a Lady
My Restless Earl
Rescued by an Earl
In the Arms of an Earl
The Reluctant Marquess (Prequel)

A Smithfield Market Regency Romance
The Smithfield Market Romances: A Sweet Regency Romance Boxset
The Rogue's Flower
Saved by the Scoundrel
Mending the Duke
The Baron's Malady

The Returned Lords of Grosvenor Square
The Returned Lords of Grosvenor Square: A Regency Romance Boxset
The Waiting Bride
The Long Return
The Duke's Saving Grace
A New Home for the Duke

The Spinsters Guild
The Spinsters Guild: A Sweet Regency Romance Boxset
A New Beginning
The Disgraced Bride
A Gentleman's Revenge
A Foolish Wager
A Lord Undone

Convenient Arrangements
Convenient Arrangements: A Regency Romance Collection
A Broken Betrothal
In Search of Love
Wed in Disgrace
Betrayal and Lies
A Past to Forget
Engaged to a Friend

Landon House
Landon House: A Regency Romance Boxset
Mistaken for a Rake
A Selfish Heart
A Love Unbroken
A Christmas Match
A Most Suitable Bride

An Expectation of Love

Second Chance Regency Romance
Second Chance Regency Romance Boxset
Loving the Scarred Soldier
Second Chance for Love
A Family of her Own
A Spinster No More

Soldiers and Sweethearts
Soldiers and Sweethearts: A Sweet Regency Romance Boxset
To Trust a Viscount
Whispers of the Heart
Dare to Love a Marquess
Healing the Earl
A Lady's Brave Heart

Ladies on their Own: Governesses and Companions
More Than a Companion
The Hidden Governess
The Companion and the Earl
More than a Governess
Protected by the Companion
A Wager with a Viscount

Lost Fortunes, Found Love
A Viscount's Stolen Fortune
For Richer, For Poorer

Christmas Stories

Christmas Kisses (Series)

The Lady's Christmas Kiss

Love and Christmas Wishes: Three Regency Romance Novellas
A Family for Christmas
Mistletoe Magic: A Regency Romance
Heart, Homes & Holidays: A Sweet Romance Anthology

Happy Reading!

All my love,

Rose

A SNEAK PEEK OF A VISCOUNT'S STOLEN FORTUNE

PROLOGUE

"What say you, Lord Foster, another round?" William tried to find some sort of inner strength by which he could answer, but there did not appear to be any available to him. "Capital. It is good that you are game."

He blinked furiously, trying to find the words to say that he did not wish to play again, and certainly had not agreed to it. But the words would not come. His jaw seemed tight, unwilling to bend to his will, and anything he wished to say died upon his closed lips.

Closing his eyes, the sounds of cards being dealt reached his ears. Yes, he had drunk a good deal, but he had not imbibed enough to make himself entirely stupid nor stupefied. Why was he struggling to even speak?

"And what shall you bet this time, Lord Foster?"

The gentleman chuckled, and William blinked again, trying to make him out. His vision was a little blurred and for whatever reason, he could not recall the name of the fellow he had sat down to play cards with. This was not his usual gambling den of course - he had come here with some friends, but now was sorely regretting it.

To that end, where were his friends? He did not recall them leaving the table. But then again, he could not remember if any of them had started a game with him, although it would be strange indeed for *all* of them to leave him to play cards alone. Given that this was a part of London none of them were familiar with, however, perhaps it was to be expected. Mayhap they had chosen to play in another gambling house or to enjoy the company of one of the ladies of the night.

My mind seems strangely clear, but I cannot seem to speak.

"If you wish to put everything on the table, then I shall not prevent you."

William shook his head no. The action caused him a little pain and he groaned only to hear the gentleman chuckle.

"Very well. You have a strong constitution, I must say. I do not think that *I* would put down everything on the table. Not if I had already lost so very much. You would be signing over almost your entire fortune to me."

Panic began to spread its way through William's heart. Somebody said something and laughed harshly, leaving the sound to echo through William's mind. He did not want to bet any longer but could not find the strength to speak.

"Shall you look at your cards, Lord Foster?"

William tried to lift a hand towards the cards that he knew were already there, but he could not find them. His fingers struck against the solid wood of the table, but, again, he could not find the cards.

"Goodness, you are a little out of sorts, are you not? Perhaps one too many brandies."

A SNEAK PEEK OF A VISCOUNT'S STOLEN FORTUNE | 195

The gentleman's harsh laugh fired William's spirits and he managed to focus on the gentleman's face for a split second. Dark eyes met his gaze and a shock of fair hair pushed back from the gentleman's brow... but then William's vision blurred again.

"I have... I have no wish to bet."

Speaking those words aloud came as a great relief to William. He had managed to say, finally, that he had no wish to continue the game.

"It is a little late, Lord Foster. You cannot pull out of the bet now."

William shook his head, squeezing his eyes closed. He was not entirely sure what game they were playing, but he had no intention of allowing this fellow to take the last bit of his money.

"No." He spoke again, the word hissing from his mouth, as though it took every bit of strength that he had to speak it. "No, I end this bet."

Somehow, he managed to push himself to his feet. A strong hand gripped his arm and William had no strength to shake it off. Everything was swirling. The room threatened to tilt itself from one side to the next, but he clung to whoever it was that held his arm. He had no intention of letting himself fall. Nausea roiled in his stomach, and he took in great breaths, swallowing hard so that he would not cast up his accounts.

"No, I make no bet. I withdraw it."

"You are not being a gentleman." The man's voice had turned hard. "A gentleman does not leave the table in such circumstances – given that I am a Viscount and you one also, it is honorable to finish the game. Perhaps you just need another brandy. It would calm your nerves."

William shook his head. That was the last thing he required.

"Gentlemen or no, I will not be continuing with this bet. I will take what I have remaining and depart." It was as if the effects of the brandy were wearing off. He could speak a little more clearly and stand now without difficulty as he let go of the other man's arm. His vision, however, remained blurry. "I will gather up the last of my things and be on my way. My friends must be nearby."

"You will sit down, and you will finish the game."

William took in a long breath - not to raise his courage, but rather to muster his strength. He wanted to *physically* leave this gambling house for good.

"I shall not." His voice shook with the effort of speaking loudly and standing without aid. "I fully intend to leave this gambling house at once, with all that I have remaining."

Whilst his resolve remained strong, William could not account for the blow that struck him on the back of the head. Evidently, his determination to leave had displeased the gentleman and darkness soon took William. His coin remained on the table and as he sank into the shadows, he could not help but fear as to what would become of it.

CHAPTER ONE

"My Lord." The gentle voice of his butler prodded William from sleep. Groaning, he turned over and buried his face in the pillow. "My Lord." Again, came the butler's voice, like an insistent prodding that jerked William into wakefulness. The moment he opened his eyes, everything screamed. "I must apologize for my insistence, but five of your closest acquaintances are in the drawing room, determined to speak with you. Lord Stoneleigh is in a somewhat injured state."

"Injured?" Keeping his eyes closed, William flung one hand over them as he turned over. "What do you mean?"

The butler cleared his throat gently.

"I believe that he has been stabbed, my Lord." The butler's voice remained calm, but his words blunt. "A surgeon has already seen to him, but his arm may be damaged permanently, I was told."

"Permanently?" The shock that flooded through William forced his eyes open as he pushed himself up on his elbows. "Are you quite certain?"

"Yes, my Lord. I did, of course, inquire whether there

was anything the gentleman needed, but he stated that the only thing required was for him to speak with you."

"And he is well?"

The butler blinked.

"As well as can be expected, my Lord."

William nodded slowly, but then wished he had not, given the pain in his head.

"Must it be at this very moment?" he moaned, as the butler looked at him, the dipping of his mouth appearing a little unsympathetic. "I do not wish to appear heartless but my head..." Squeezing his eyes closed, he let out a heavy sigh. "Can they not wait until I am a little recovered?"

The butler shook his head.

"I apologize, my Lord, but I was told that they wish to speak to you urgently and that they would not leave until they had spoken with you. That is why I came to you at once. It appears most severe indeed."

"I see." William realized that he had no other choice but to rise, pushing one hand through his hair as the pain in his head grew. "This is most extraordinary. Whatever is it that they wish to speak to me about so urgently?"

"I could not say, my Lord." The butler stood dutifully back as William tried to rise from his bed. "Your valet is waiting outside the door; shall I fetch him?"

"Yes." William's head was pounding, and he grimaced as he attempted to remove his legs from the sheets. They appeared to be tangled in them, and it took him some time to extricate himself, hampered entirely by the pain in his head. "I am sure that, after last night, my friends must also be feeling the effects of a little too much enjoyment," he muttered aloud. "Why then-"

Shock tore through him as he suddenly realized that he could not recall what had happened the previous evening.

He could not even remember how he had made his way home. A heaviness dropped into the pit of his stomach, although there was no explanation for why he felt such a thing. Had something happened last night that he had forgotten about?

"Jefferies." Moving forward so that his valet could help him dress, William glanced at his butler who had been on his way out the door. "You may speak freely. Was I in something of a sorry state when I returned home last evening?"

There was no flicker of a smile in the butler's eyes. His expression remained entirely impassive.

"No, my Lord, you were not in your cups. You were entirely unconscious."

William blinked rapidly.

"Unconscious?"

The butler nodded.

"Yes, my Lord."

"Are you quite sure?"

The butler lifted one eyebrow.

"Yes, my Lord. The carriage arrived, but no one emerged. Your coachman and I made certain that you were safe in your bed very soon afterward, however."

Confusion marred William's brow. It was most unlike him to drink so very much that he became lost in drunkenness. He could not recall the last time he had done so. A little merry, perhaps, but never to the point of entirely losing his consciousness.

How very strange.

Shoving his fingers through his short, dark hair in an attempt to soothe the ache, William winced suddenly as his fingers found a rather large bump on the side of his head. Wincing, he traced it gingerly.

That certainly was not there yesterday.

It seemed that the pain in his head was not from drinking a little too much, but rather from whatever had collided with his head. A little concerned that he had been involved in some sort of fight – again, entirely out of character for him – he now wondered if his friends were present to make certain that he was either quite well or willing to take on whatever consequences now faced him. William urged his valet to hurry. *Did not my butler say that Lord Stoneleigh was injured? Surely, I could not have been the one to do such a thing as that!*

"I am glad to see you a little recovered, my Lord." The butler's voice remained a dull monotone. "Should I bring you something to drink? Refreshments were offered to your acquaintances, but they were refused."

"Coffee, please."

The pain in his head was lingering still, in all its strength, but William ignored it. A new sense of urgency settled over him as he hurried from his bedchamber and made his way directly to the drawing room. Conversation was already taking place as he stepped inside, only to stop dead as he entered the room. His five acquaintances, whom he had stepped out with the previous evening, all turned to look at him as one. Fear began to tie itself around William's heart.

"Lord Stoneleigh." William put out one hand towards his friend. "You are injured, my butler tells me."

His friend nodded but his eyes remained a little wide.

"I am, but that is not the reason we are here. We must know if you are in the same situation as we all find ourselves at present?"

The question made very little sense to William, and he took a moment to study Lord Stoneleigh before turning to the rest of his friends.

"The same situation?" he repeated. "Forgive me, I do not understand."

"We should never have set foot in that seedy place." Lord Thornbridge pushed one hand through his hair, adding to its disarray. Silently, William considered that it appeared as though Lord Thornbridge had been doing such a thing for many hours. "It was I who became aware of it first. I spoke to the others, and they are all in the same situation. You are the only one we have not yet spoken to."

"I do not understand what you mean." More confused than ever, William spread his hands. "What situation is it that you speak of?"

It was Lord Wiltsham who spoke first. Every other gentleman was staring at William as though they had some dreadful news to impart but did not quite know how to say it.

"My friend, we have lost our fortunes."

Shock poured into William's heart. He stared back at Lord Wiltsham uncomprehendingly.

"Your fortunes?"

"Yes. Some more, some less but a good deal of wealth is gone from us all."

William closed his eyes, his chest tight. How could this be?

"He does not know." William's eyes flew open, swinging towards Lord Pottinger as he looked at the others. "He cannot tell us either."

"Tell you?" William's voice was hoarse. "What is it that you mean? How can you have lost your fortunes? What is it you were expecting to hear from me?"

He stared at one gentleman, then moved his gaze to the next. These gentlemen were his friends, and how they could have lost so much coin in one evening was incomprehensible to him. They were not foolish gentlemen. Yes, they enjoyed cards and gambling and the like on occasion, but they would never have been so lacking in wisdom, regardless of how much they had imbibed.

"Some of us do not wish to say it, but it is true." Lord Silverton glanced at William, then looked away. "We have realized that our fortunes have been lost. Some have a little more left than others, but we are now in great difficulty."

William shook his head.

"It cannot be. You are all gentlemen with wisdom running through you. You would not behave so without consideration! I cannot believe that you have all willingly set your coin into the hands of others. You would not do such a thing to your family name."

Lord Stoneleigh was the next to speak.

"I fear you may also be in the same situation, my friend." His eyes were dull, his face pale – although mayhap that came from his injury. "You are correct that we are gentlemen of wisdom, but making our way to that part of London last evening was not wise. It appears that certain gentlemen - or those masquerading as gentlemen - have taken our coin from us in ways that are both unscrupulous and unfair."

Fire tore through William as he again shook his head.

"I would never give away my fortune to the point of poverty," he declared determinedly. "I am certain I would not have done so."

"As we thought also." Lord Pottinger threw up his hands. "But you find us now without fortune, leaving us struggling for the remainder of our days. That is, unless we can find a way to recover it from those unscrupulous sorts who have taken it from us... although how we are to prove that they have done so is quite beyond me."

William took a deep breath. He was quite certain that he would never have behaved in such a foolish way as was being suggested, but the fear that lingered in his friend's eyes was enough to unsettle him. If it was as they said, then he might well discover himself to be in the same situation as they.

"I am quite sure that I cannot..." Trailing off at the heaviness in each of his friend's eyes, William sighed, nodded, and rose to his feet. "I will have my man of business discover the truth," he declared, as his friends glanced at each other. "It *cannot* be as you say. I would certainly never..."

A sudden gasp broke from his lips as the memories began to pour into his mind. He recalled why the pain in his head was so severe, remembered the gentleman who had insisted upon him betting, even though William had been somehow unable to speak. A memory of attempting to declare that he would not bet anymore forced its way into his mind – as well as the pain in his head which had come swiftly thereafter.

"You remember now, I think." Lord Wiltsham's smile was rueful. "Something happened, did it not?"

William began to nod slowly, his heart pounding furiously in his chest.

"It is as I feared." Lord Wiltsham sighed and looked away. "We have all been taken in by someone. I do not know who, for it appears to be different for each of us. Going to that east part of London – to those 'copper hells' instead of our own gambling houses - has made a difficult path for all of us now. We have very little fortune left to speak of."

"But I did not wish to gamble." Hearing his voice hoarse, William closed his eyes. Thoughts were pouring into his mind, but he could make very little sense of them. "I told him I did not wish to gamble."

"Then perhaps you did not." A faint note of hope entered Lord Wiltsham's voice. "Mayhap you remain free of this injury."

William opened his eyes and looked straight at his friend.

"No, I do not believe I am." The truth brought fresh pain to his heart. "I remember now that someone injured me. I do not recall anything after that, but my butler informs me that I arrived home in an unconscious state. If it is as you say, then I am sure that whoever I was playing cards with made certain that they stole a great deal of coin. Lifting his hand, he pinched the bridge of his nose. "Perhaps I have lost everything."

"I will be blunt with you, my friend." Lord Thornbridge's eyes were clear, but his words brought fear. "It sounds as though you will discover that you *have* lost a great deal. It may not be everything, but it will certainly be enough to change the course of your life from this day forward."

The frankness with which he spoke was difficult for William to hear. He wanted to awaken all over again, to imagine that this day was not as it seemed.

"We ought never to have left our usual haunts." Lord Pottinger dropped his face into his hands, his words muffled. "In doing so, we appear to have been taken advantage of by those who pretended to be naught but gentlemen."

"They have done more than take advantage." William's voice was hoarse. "I recall that I did not feel well last night. My vision was blurred, and I do not even remember the gentleman's face. And yet somehow, I have managed to lose my fortune to him. My behavior does not make sense, and nor does any of yours." Silence filled the room as he stretched his hands out wide, looking at each one in turn.

Lord Thornbridge was the first to speak in response.

"You believe that this was deliberate. You think that these... scoundrels... gave us something to make us lose our senses?"

"In my case, I am certain that they did." William bit his lip. "I cannot give you a clear explanation for it, but I am quite certain that I would never have behaved in such a manner. The responsibility of the title has been heavy on my shoulders for many years, and I would never have given such a fortune away."

"Nor would I. But yet it seems that I have done so." Lord Pottinger shook his head. "I cannot see any recourse."

"And yet it is there." William took a step closer, refusing to give in to the dread which threatened to tear away every single shred of determination that tried to enter his heart. "The only way we will regain our fortune is to find those responsible, and demand that they return our coin to us. I will not stand by and allow myself to lose what should see me through the remainder of my days – and to set my heir in good standing!"

His friends did not immediately reply. None answered with hope nor expectation, for they all shook their heads and looked away as though they were quite lost in fear and darkness. William could feel it clutching at him also, but he refused to allow its spindly fingers to tighten around his neck.

"We have each lost our fortune in different ways." Lord Thornbridge shrugged, then dropped his shoulders. "However are we supposed to find those responsible, when we were all in differing situations?"

William spread his hands.

"I cannot say as yet, but there must be something that each of us can do to find out who is to blame. Otherwise, the future of our lives remains rather bleak."

A sudden thought of Lady Florence filled his mind. He had been about to ask for her hand, but should he tell her about what had occurred, then William was quite certain that she would refuse him. After all, no young lady would consider a gentleman who had no fortune.

His heart sank.

"You are right." Lord Wiltsham's voice had a tad more confidence and William lifted his head. "We cannot sit here and simply accept that our fortunes are gone, not if we believe that they have been unfairly taken. Instead, we must do all we can to find the truth and to recover whatever coin we can."

"I agree." Lord Stoneleigh tried to spread his hands, then winced with the pain from his injury. "I simply do not know how to go about it."

"That will take some time, and I would suggest that you give yourself a few days to recover from the shock and to think about what must be done." Lord Thornbridge now also appeared to be willing to follow William's lead. "Since I have very little coin left, I must make changes to my household immediately – and I shall have to return to my estate to do it. Thereafter, however, I will consider what I shall do to find out where my fortune has gone. Perhaps we can encourage each other, sharing any news about what we have discovered with each other."

"Yes, I quite agree." Letting out a slow breath, William considered what he would now face. It would be difficult, certainly, yet he was prepared. He knew how society would treat him once news about his lack of funds was discovered and William would have to find the mental strength to face it. What was important to him at present was that he found the perpetrators, for that was the only way he could see to regain some of his fortune – and his standing in society.

"I should speak to my man of business at once." William dropped his head and blew out a huff of breath before he lifted it again. "This will not be a pleasant time, gentlemen. But at least we have the companionship and encouragement of each other as we face this dreadful circumstance together."

His friends nodded, but no one smiled. A heavy sense of gloom penetrated the air and William's heart threatened to sink lower still as he fought to cling to his hope that he would restore his fortune soon enough.

I will find out who did this. And I shall not remain in their grip for long.

Oh my! How terrible for Lord Wiltsham! And there is more bad news to come regarding his betrothed…or should I say former betrothed? Let's hope he can find a way out this mess! A Viscount's Stolen Fortune

JOIN MY MAILING LIST

Sign up for my newsletter to stay up to date on new releases, contests, giveaways, freebies, and deals!

Free book with signup!

Facebook Giveaways! Books and Amazon gift cards! Join me on Facebook: https://www.facebook.com/rosepearsonauthor

Join my new Facebook group! Rose's Ravenous Readers

Website: www.RosePearsonAuthor.com

Follow me on Goodreads: Author Page

You can also follow me on Bookbub! Click on the picture below – see the Follow button?

210 | JOIN MY MAILING LIST

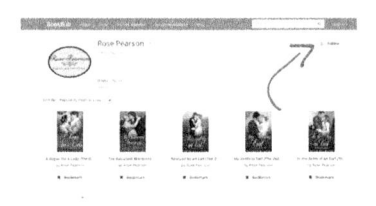